the
Palm Beach
Wedding
Gone Awry

Thank God It's Friday Series
Book One

MERRIE VOLLMER

Contents

– One –
A Happy Reunion

ON A WEDNESDAY AFTERNOON IN OCTOBER, the light gray clouds that hung over the majestic Breakers Palm Beach resort parted, exposing a bright blue sky and brilliant sunshine. The sunlight intensified the color of the red brick driveway leading up to the opulent hotel's entrance. It made the cascading water in the massive Renaissance fountain sparkle, and it accentuated the verdant color of the immaculate tropical landscape.

In a quiet corner of the outdoor courtyard, Lady Friday-Stone welcomed the sunlight. She felt the warm rays of dappled sunshine on her skin as she sipped her mango flavored iced tea and slowly turned the pages of her magazine. She did not feel like going to the beach. She did not feel like people watching in the lobby. She did not feel like notifying her younger sister, Deidre, the mother of the bride, that she had arrived.

Even though she made the drive from her home on the west coast of Florida to Palm Beach alone, she still felt the need for more time to herself before the craziness began. She would wait for support from her best friend and sister-in-law, Frances Friday. She breathed in a full breath and let it out slowly. She smelled a wonderful combination of salty ocean air and tropical sunscreen. Was the fragrance mango or coconut or a combination of both, she wondered.

Her brother Sam's wife, Frances, had a magical effect on the Friday family. She brought common sense and decisive action to whatever confusing or often frantic problem they were facing. Frances could win the award for the most loved in-law on the planet if such an award existed. When she arrived at family events, the Friday relatives often said to one another, "Thank God it's Frances Friday." Yes, she would wait for Frances.

Lady did not have to wait long. A tall brunette dressed in black athletic wear walked energetically into the courtyard. Her enthusiastic voice and warm smile caused not only Lady, but also others seated in the courtyard to look up and take notice.

"I thought I would find you in a quiet corner with a magazine and a glass of tea," said Frances as she took a seat at the table. "Have you seen Deidre yet?"

"No, not yet," Lady said with a tinge of guilt in her voice. "I'm sure she is busy with wedding stuff and I wanted to wait for you. How was your drive over from St. Petersburg?"

Frances said, "I made good time. I came straight from my meeting in Tampa. It's a good thing we were both able to come a few days early. I'm sure the wedding plans are going well but if not, we can jump in and help with any last minute glitches." Knowing her in-laws, Frances was assuming that there would naturally be last minute glitches. She was actually hoping there were some complications during the weekend. She thrived on solving problems and helping people. Her husband did not need her the next few days. He was working on an important case and could not get away until just before the wedding ceremony. Her four children did not need her in the next few days. Their schedules were full with job and school responsibilities and none of them could make it to Palm Beach until the day of the wedding.

Frances was in between careers. She was trying to start a business but that was still in the dream stage and did not require all her energy. This weekend she had time and she wanted to feel useful.

Lady put her fingers in her ears and said, "La, la, la. I can't hear you. You know I don't want to know anything about the wedding plans. I don't want to hear about any problems. I just want to take this weekend as it comes and not think about the million ways it could have been planned better. You know I love my sister, but she is so unorganized."

"Deidre is wonderful and being organized is not the most important thing. She has such a passionate, free-flowing, creative spirit. I can't wait to see what she has dreamed up for the wedding."

"Yes, that is what our mother called it, but I think that was just a kind way of saying Deidre is an overly emotional scatterbrain."

"You are so hard on your family. I think they are all very interesting people in their own way. Are you looking forward to seeing your brother Thomas and little Alexandra?"

"Little Alexandra! She must be eighteen years old by now. I hope she remembers us. Poor girl was shipped off to that boarding school and not allowed to see our family all this time. I think Brittany did it to spite all of us. It was the stuff of fairy tales. Wicked stepmothers and innocent girls locked away in towers. I'm surprised that marriage lasted ten years. I tried to warn him."

Lady had been outspoken when her brother started dating so soon after his first wife's death. She even took him to see Hamlet at the theatre and poked him in the ribs with her elbow when Hamlet said, "See how the funeral's baked meats did coldly furnish forth the marriage tables" indicating that she, and others, thought that the marriage was too hasty. The family was not sure that Brittany was a good match for Thomas and suspected that she was after his money. He did marry Brittany and she picked up on the family's hesitation. She made them pay through various emotional stratagems, mainly isolating Thomas and his daughter from them.

Frances could hear the anger and pain in Lady's voice. She knew she was overly protective of her older brother and saddened by the rift in the relationship. She focused on the present instead of the past. "I am sorry Thomas is divorced but am very happy the Friday family ban is lifted. I can't wait to reconnect with Alexandra. It has been too long."

"When is your family arriving?" asked Lady. "James

and my girls will be here right before the wedding on Saturday. Albert can't make it. He is still in England."

"Same with my family," agreed Frances with disappointment in her voice. "Sam is working on a big case and my kids are busy. They won't be here until right before the wedding on Saturday. I miss the days when they were young and went everywhere with us. Life was so simple and predictable then."

As Frances ordered an iced tea, Lady appraised her sister-in-law's outfit. It did not fit amidst the tropical surroundings. Lady had chosen an expensive shift dress in a bright tropical print for her entrance to The Breakers. She had carefully planned and packed the perfect wardrobe for the weekend wedding in Palm Beach. Exactly one week before the wedding she had her short blond hair cut and highlighted to perfection. She showed her hairdresser her Pinterest board of famous actresses who wore their hair short. She was also careful to whiten her teeth and get some sun on her skin before the big wedding. She was not a vain person; she just liked to be prepared.

Frances's outfit bothered her, and she voiced her irritation. "Frances, why are you wearing black athletic clothes? We are at a high-end tropical resort. You have been wearing black a lot lately. I think you are subconsciously in mourning. I bet it is because you just became an empty nester."

"Don't be ridiculous," said Frances. "I'm not in mourning. Have you been listening to that psychology podcast again?"

"I know you Frances. Since Faith went off to college,

you have not been your usual self and every time I see you, you are wearing black. I hope you are not wearing black to the wedding?"

Frances loved wearing trendy athletic wear not because she was trendy or athletic, but because she was just very practical. She considered Lady's comment. Maybe she did tend to wear too much black. Or maybe she was becoming a lazy dresser. She was a little melancholy that her youngest child went to college and the house was noticeably empty.

Being an optimist and not a person to dwell on unhappy thoughts, she told herself she was excited about this new phase of life. No! Lady was wrong, and Frances corrected her. "I am wearing black because it is so versatile, not because I am depressed. I like to travel in my black athletic wear because it is comfortable and it doesn't wrinkle. Besides the artist Renoir said, 'I've been forty years discovering that the queen of all colors is black,' and I agree with him."

Frances added, "I told you, don't call me an empty nester. I don't like that term. It sounds so grim and hopeless. Why can't we call it 'new chapter' or 'next adventure' or 'extra closet space'? Maybe women wouldn't be depressed when their children leave home if they called it something more positive and hopeful."

Lady was not convinced. "Are you wearing a black dress to the wedding? What about the rehearsal dinner? What are you wearing for that? You know they have a Lilly Pulitzer store here if you need something bright and beachy."

"I'm wearing a white leather miniskirt and an eighties track jacket with engineer boots," Frances replied. "Why are you so worried about my wardrobe?"

"You know Ella hates black," Lady reminded her. "She said the other day on her Instagram post that she thinks wearing black in South Florida is depressing. She got three thousand likes on her post. I don't want the bride to be depressed this weekend. You know how emotional Ella and her mother can be."

Frances looked past Lady and noticed a tall young girl wearing black jeans and a black hoodie standing alone, almost hiding, in an archway. She looked uncomfortably out of place.

"There is someone else wearing black," said Frances as she jumped up and approached the young girl. She stretched her arms out and said, "Alexandra, do you remember me? I am your Aunt Frances."

"Hello, Aunt Frances," said the niece, giving her aunt an awkward side hug.

"Oh child, please call me Aunt Franny, or as you used to say when you were five years old, 'Aunt Fwanny.'"

Alexandra pulled the hoodie off her head revealing her thick, dark brown hair. She favored her Greek mother with her dark eyes and olive complexion. However, after spending so many years in the north, she had the pale, translucent skin that plagues people who don't see the sun very often. She was tall compared to most girls, but her high school volleyball coach was disappointed that her height did not extend beyond five feet nine inches.

"Is this Alexandra?" said Lady, gently clasping her

hands around Alexandra's face. "Well my goodness gracious, you are growing into the spitting image of your mother."

Lady looked up and down the lobby and said, "Where is your father?"

"I don't know," said Alexandra. "He was right behind me. He must have wandered off again. He is always doing that. It is so annoying."

While the three women were getting into a lively conversation, Alexandra's father, Thomas Friday, wandered up to the happy reunion. He was trailing behind, as usual, having stopped to closely examine each palm, tropical plant, and flower arrangement as he entered the hotel's grand lobby.

Thomas was an attractive man but no one could tell. Underneath his unkempt hair, crumpled clothes and hunched over posture was a tall, fit man that looked good for his age. He wore expensive name brand clothes that his previous wife bought for him but no one would mistake him for a well-dressed man. His shirt and pants were always wrinkled like he had slept in them. His thick, wavy, brown hair rarely encountered a barber's tools.

His tardiness may have irritated his teenage daughter but his sister and sister-in-law were neither surprised nor annoyed. Frances and Lady gave Thomas long overdue hugs. Lady's eyes started to water but she quickly wiped them and said in her characteristically blunt way, "Hello, brother, I'm am sorry to hear about your failed marriage although anyone could have seen that coming.

You should have listened to us. Oh well, at least you are here with us now."

Thomas also had trouble holding back tears, and his eyes became moist. "I regret that Brittany did not like to spend time with our family. Lady, I know you love to hear it so I will say it. You were right. I should have listened to you. Brittany was not right for me. I think she married me for my money and my money is what she got." Thomas was uncomfortable with emotional scenes, so he added a joke to lighten the mood. "After the divorce, I am so broke, I can't even afford to pay attention."

Frances smiled and mused to herself that Thomas Friday had trouble paying attention when he had plenty of money at his disposal. Still, why point that out now. That would be unkind. A person should be sympathetic in these situations. Frances kindly interjected, "Yes, Thomas, we are sorry you had to go through a terrible divorce. We will support you and Alexandra in any way we can. Families must stick together."

Talking about his life mistakes made Thomas uncomfortable, so he changed the subject. He asked, "Did you notice the exquisite collection of orchids that they have at this hotel?"

"No, Thomas. I uh, did not really take in the flowers quite yet. I was thinking about seeing long-lost relatives," said Frances.

"Long-lost relatives? Where? Here?" said Thomas, looking around the lobby for any familiar faces and then slowly realizing she was referring to him. "Oh, yes, of course we are the long-lost relatives. Now I see what you mean."

"Thomas, you haven't changed a bit," said Frances, glancing sympathetically at Alexandra, who was rolling her eyes.

Thomas smiled and subconsciously patted his stomach. He thought Frances was referring to his physical appearance not having altered over the years. He had to admit he was flattered by her comment. He had always liked Frances.

While the two aunts and niece continued catching up on ten years, Thomas's mind wandered. It often wandered when women were talking. He looked past them admiring the areca palms lining the courtyard gently swaying in the breeze. Or were they lady palms? He would have to look it up when he had time. One of the palms started trembling violently. Thomas left the conversation to have a closer look. As he approached the quivering palm, he heard a distinct, "Psst" sound. Again, the palm said, "Psst, Thomas, is that you?" He was naturally perplexed. He was in the habit of speaking to his plants, but he had never had one speak to him. Moving in closer, he saw that hiding behind the palm was a petite woman in a plush white robe with green goo on her face and something like cucumber slices on her forehead.

"Thomas, I need you to do me a favor," said the woman, with urgency in her voice.

"Certainly, Miss. I'd be happy to help," said Thomas courteously.

"Miss, what do you mean Miss? It's Deidre, your

sister, you imbecile. Something terrible has happened and I need you to call Frances over here."

"Deidre!" said Thomas with brotherly affection. "I did not recognize you at first. How are you? You are look-ing … er … uh, well."

"Thomas! Go get Frances now."

Thomas walked back to the middle of the courtyard and pointed in the direction of the palm tree. "Deidre would like to speak to you, Frances."

"Where is she? How do you know she wants me?" asked Frances.

"She just told me. For some reason, she is stand-ing behind that palm tree over there in a bath robe," he explained.

Neither Lady nor Frances was fazed by this infor-mation, knowing their sister as they did. Alexandra was the only family member surprised by his explanation. All four relatives huddled up to the potted palm.

"Deidre, what is going on and what are you doing hiding there?" asked Frances.

"I was in the spa getting my mother of the bride beauty treatment. When I ran out the back door of the spa, I got locked out. Luckily I spotted you here and made my way over hiding behind the landscape. I can't be seen like this. You have to help me," she said, exasperated.

Lady said, "I don't even want to ask. Why did you run out of the spa?"

Deidre became weepy as she explained to her sym-pathetic family members. The expensive botanical mask began to slide off her face and she wiped it on her robe. "Ella texted me while I was in the spa. This is awful. I don't know what to do."

Deidre Friday wasted her money on expensive spa facials. She was born with fair, well-hydrated skin that never produced blemishes or spots. She applied sunscreen liberally and kept out of the sun as much as possible. Her curly strawberry blonde hair showed only slight hints of her age with a few wispy white hairs here and there. Her whole appearance was youthful. Even the middle age weight gain under her chin and in her midsection did not seem to age her. She did not focus on her body and she did not give a whit about her weight.

"Tell us exactly what happened," said Frances.

Deidre stood up straight, took a deep breath, and began a very long sentence. "Ella wants to call off the wedding because she had a fight with Auden and says she hates him now and she won't talk to me even though I tried to be understanding and positive and now she has locked herself in the bathroom in our suite and says she won't come out until Tuesday after everyone has gone home."

She gasped for air and continued with another very long sentence. "I can't call off the wedding after all the time and money we've spent and what will the guests think and Ella will be an old maid and live with me forever and probably want to have cats and you know I am allergic to cats."

Lady said, "Deidre, get a hold of yourself. Stop and take a breath."

Deidre obeyed her older sister and took a deep breath and said in a calmer voice, "You have to come up to our suite and help. I know you can get her to come out of the bathroom and talk to us."

Frances said, "We will all do our best. Lady and Alexandra, you go open the spa back door to let Deidre in. Thomas and I will head up to the room."

Lady and Alexandra followed Deidre as she darted from potted plant to potted plant making her way back to the spa without attracting attention. Once they assisted her unnoticed back to the spa, they headed to the suite.

Lady asked Alexandra as they walked, "Are you happy to be back in Florida after all this time? What have you been doing since high school graduation?"

"I guess I'm am happy. I've only been here a few days. I worked at a volleyball camp all summer up north and then I traveled out west with some friends. It was a graduation present from my dad."

"Are you and your father reconnecting—you know after the divorce?"

"I guess we are. I did not feel very connected to begin with. I was away most of the time and when I was home, Brittany was always around and involved in everything we did. I don't think I ever spoke with my dad without her being there. Our drive over today was the first time in a long time that we were alone. It was kind of weird.

We did not really talk about much." Alexandra stopped. She was uneasy talking about her relationship with her father because she had not really figured it out yet. She was entering a new phase of life in a new location with a new way of looking at her family relationships. Also, she really did not want to talk about her dad's ex-wife, Brittany.

She decided to ask her aunt a question instead. "I always wanted to know why your name is Lady. Is it a nickname?"

Lady was happy to change the subject. She thought that perhaps her last question was too direct and personal. After all, she had not seen her niece since she was eight years old, and she did not want to be intrusive. She said proudly, "My full name is Laodicea Elizabeth Friday-Stone. My mother heard the name Laodicea during one of her infrequent visits to church and decided it was the perfect name for her first daughter. Later, however, she realized that the name did not have a good meaning in the Scriptures so she shortened my name to Lady, not wanting any trouble with the Man Upstairs. I like my name. It suits me. It sounds very British doesn't it? I'm one of those women who idolize everything British. I drink tea every day and follow the royal family closely."

Thomas stopped at the elevator with Frances. He said, "I don't have any experience extracting distressed brides

from bathrooms so I think I will go read my book before dinner. I wanted to ask you something before you go up."

Frances looked at her brother-in-law curiously. He had a pained, almost guilty look on his face. She asked, "What is it, Thomas?"

"I'm anxious for you to spend time with Alexandra. She needs a role model in her life now. She has been through a lot and I don't always know how to talk to her."

"I'll take her under my wing and look out for her this weekend. We will be fast friends again in no time. It will be like we were never apart."

Thomas looked relieved. "She has only been in Florida a few days, so she may not have any appropriate clothes for this weekend. She wore uniforms at the boarding school and I think she bought most of her clothes at a thrift store. Brittany was not very generous with her and kept her on a tight budget." Fumbling in his pocket and retrieving his wallet he handed her his credit card. "Buy her what she wants. Whatever she wants," he repeated with the guilt that comes from a man who has not been there enough for his only child.

Frances knew that buying things would not mend their relationship, but it was a start. She could tell that he was making an effort to be a better father and she admired him for it. She took the credit card and assured him that Alexandra would have what she needed. She was actually more excited than she would have expected at the thought of taking her niece shopping. It was one thing she had always enjoyed doing with her daughters but now their trips were less frequent. She asked, "What

kind of budget are we talking about for her new Florida wardrobe?"

"I don't really have number in mind. The poor girl has worked so hard in school with very few perks or enjoyments. I trust your judgment. And also, I didn't have a chance to get a wedding present for Ella and Otto. Do you think you could get a nice gift for them while you are out?"

"The groom's name is Auden, not Otto. Of course, I'd be happy to pick out a gift for you. Don't worry about a thing."

Thomas walked down the loggia to find a quiet spot to read, and Frances headed to the suite to help reason with the bride-to-be.

– Two –
The Old Girlfriend

IN THE MONTH OF JULY PRECEDING THE WEDDING, July eleventh to be precise, the mother of the groom left her sprawling farm in Alachua County and headed into town on an important errand. She drove her pickup truck down the lonely country road past green fields where cattle were grazing and enjoying shade under the spreading branches of large live oaks. She passed several horse farms with inquisitive horses hanging their heads over the split rail fence, swishing flies off their backs with their tails while they watched her drive by.

Driving through this peaceful, bucolic, scene, Betsy Woods felt fairly content. Their farm was doing better than previous years due to recent organic food and farm to table trends. They had their health, and in a few months her only son was getting married. Betsy's dream had always been for Auden to marry a local girl and take over the family farm. She had to let that dream go. Auden was marrying a girl who was very different from her expectations and the couple would most likely live in Palm Beach. As her truck bumped along the road she mused, "It's funny how things turn out completely different than you imagine." And she concluded, "This happened because he went off to that fancy college." She clearly remembered the conversation following Auden's graduation from high school.

Auden had pleaded with his parents. "I want to go to college out of state. I want to go somewhere up north where there is cold weather and a change of seasons."

His parents would try to reason with him. "Why do you want to go out of state? The tuition is more than double and there are so many good schools in Florida. You should go to University of Florida and major in horticulture science."

"I don't want to stay in Florida," he protested. "And I don't want to be a farmer."

"Why do you want to leave Florida? Why do you want to go so far away?"

"I want to go somewhere where everyone in the town does not know me, where I can meet new, interesting, and different people."

"People outside of Florida are not that interesting," they would assure him.

"I have lived here all my life and I am tired of everything being the same."

"People are people wherever you go, except maybe California—they are definitely different there," they would say with the wisdom that comes from a long life of knowing people. And on and on and round and round the conversation went until he stormed out of the room completely frustrated at not getting his point across to his parents.

Auden's parents finally relented. "Let the prodigal son go," they thought, "and he will come to his senses one day and return home to Florida."

Betsy was so absorbed in her thoughts that she did not heed the speed limit sign as she neared the town. Almost immediately she heard a police siren and saw flashing lights behind her.

She rolled down the window. "Hello, Roy. Sorry, I wasn't paying attention. Do you have to ticket me?"

"Well I guess I'll let you slide this time," said the officer and long-time friend. "By the way, I never told you congratulations. I hear Auden is getting hitched soon. Who's the lucky girl?"

"Her name is Ella Birnam. He met her at Hanlon, the college in North Carolina."

"How are the wedding plans going?"

"Good, I guess. The bride and her mother are doing everything. I just have to hire the deejay. I haven't found one yet. They are all so expensive down there in Palm Beach."

"Palm Beach!" said Roy raising his eyebrows. "Sounds like a fancy wedding."

"I'm sure it will be. Ella and her mother like to spend money. They are not very down-to-earth people—they got so much money they don't know what to do with it."

Roy scratched his chin and thought about his son, who was a junior in high school. He wondered if he should send him to Hanlon to meet a rich girl. He made a mental note to discuss it with his wife when he got home. He added, "I always thought Auden would marry Debbie Stewart. They were always together, and didn't they date on and off since middle school?"

"Yes. I thought they would end up together, too, but as soon as he got to Hanlon, he broke up with her. She was really hurt. She was so attached to Auden, almost obsessed with him. Unfortunately, I think she was part of the 'sameness' that he was trying to get away from."

"Sometimes small-town kids want to get away and figure out who they are. At least he came back to Florida," Roy said, trying to add a silver lining to the conversation. "My granny always used to say, 'You can take the boy out of Florida but you can't take the Florida out of the boy.'"

Auden's plan was to take the boy out of Florida as soon as he graduated from high school. He left everything and everyone behind him as he drove his pickup truck to college. He did not break up with his girlfriend before he left for college because that would have been hard to do, and his immaturity caused him to avoid situations that made him uncomfortable. One week into his first semester at Hanlon, he broke up with Debbie. Not being a person to beat around the bush, he texted her in as few characters as possible to get his meaning across. He did not like messy emotional texting. It was too draining on him.

"Hey Debbie – it's over," read his succinct text.

"What do you mean it's over? Did you already meet someone else? Your Facebook still says 'in a relationship,'" she texted back with a surprised face emoji.

Reading her text, he thought, "What does this girl want from me?" He decided to put in the effort and compose complete sentences in his next text to show that he was not entirely heartless. Auden texted back, "I have tried to make this long-distance relationship work, but it is too hard. I want to date other people. Don't text me anymore."

Naturally Debbie was devastated, but she did not fall on a knife or drink poison, as tragic Shakespearean female leads are apt to do. She refused to believe that Auden was breaking up with her. She was confident that Auden would tire of college girls, see his mistake and come back to her. Four years later, she still held out hope.

There is a wide spectrum of reactions when a person is not the one chosen for the happily ever after. On one end of the spectrum you have someone like the character Eponine in *Les Miserables*, who keeps her love for Marius to herself and pines for him throughout the story. She even dies for him without ever expressing her deep devotion.

On the other end of the spectrum you have the character Julianne from the movie *My Best Friend's Wedding*. Julianne attends a wedding with the sole purpose of declaring her love for the groom at the last minute and wrecking the impending marriage. Debbie Stewart fell much closer on the spectrum to Julianne's character, and she was devising a similar plan.

The first and most critical step in her plan was to somehow get invited to the wedding. On July eleventh, she was sure that Auden's mother, who was known for her frugality, would come into town for a free Slurpee at 7-Eleven. She camped out at the local store and, true to her predictions, Betsy's truck pulled into the parking lot. Debbie walked over to the Slurpee machine and struck up a conversation.

"Hello, Mrs. Woods," she said with the sweetest voice she could muster.

"Well, hello, Debbie, how are you? Are you here to get your free Slurpee?"

"No, I don't really like them. They are too cold and give me a brain freeze headache," said Debbie.

"Well, can I have yours then?" said Mrs. Woods handing her a large cup to fill. "Here fill this up. It is only one free Slurpee per person."

As Debbie filled the cup with frozen Coke she changed the subject away from Slurpees, "I bet you're excited for the upcoming wedding."

"Yes. We're really looking forward to it," said Mrs. Woods concentrating on her task. She was a little surprised that Debbie was so chatty and wanted to talk about her former boyfriend's wedding.

"How is the wedding planning going? I can't imagine planning a wedding," said Debbie disingenuously. She had imagined planning a wedding with Auden many times and had a Pinterest board to prove it. "I imagine the bride and groom are stressed out about all the things that have to be done before the wedding. I bet it is taking a toll on their relationship."

"No, not really. Ella's family is doing everything, and Auden does not have to do much except show up with his groomsmen a few days before the wedding. And frankly, I don't think her family wants our help," said Betsy with a little resentment in her voice.

"Wow. I can't believe they won't let you help with your son's wedding," said Debbie, trying to drive a wedge between future in-laws.

"Nope. They are even doing the rehearsal dinner. They only asked for one thing. Ella wants Auden to find a deejay for the reception since he knows more about music than she does."

There it was—Debbie's ticket to the wedding. She was not given the opportunity to go to college. However, she was blessed with musical talent so, right after high school, she started a deejay business. She had that rare combination found in an artist of both creativity and enterprise, and as a result her deejay business was very successful.

They walked outside together and Debbie handed her the Slurpee. She knew she had to act fast or this opportunity would be gone. Knowing Mrs. Woods fondness for saving money, she boldly offered, "You know my deejay business is going really well, and I am usually very busy in October, but I would be glad to do Auden's wedding for basically free since our families are old friends."

"Won't that be a little awkward?" said Mrs. Woods. "I mean, since you and Auden dated?"

"No! Pa-shaw! Please. That was years ago. We are totally fine. Really, I would love to be there and do what I can to make it a memorable night for Auden."

Mrs. Woods was still thinking about the "basically free" phrase. She mulled it over in her mind. It might be a little awkward, but where would she find another dee-jay at such a good price? Also, Debbie was practically part of the family. She made a quick decision. "Well, Debbie, you are hired. I will send you the information."

Debbie squealed, "Yes! Thank You!" Lowering her voice to normal level, she added, "You know what would be fun, is if you didn't tell Auden that I'm the deejay. We could surprise him. He would be like 'What? Debbie's the deejay? Mom, what a great idea.'"

As Betsy drove away sipping her Slurpee she wondered if hiring Auden's old girlfriend was a good idea. She also wondered if surprising him was wise. She shrugged it off and thought, "If hiring Auden's old girlfriend is a problem, that's not my fault. If they're going to exclude me from the wedding planning, I'm not responsible for the outcome." She would let the wheel of fortune spin and see what happened if Ella found out about Debbie and Auden's past.

Having secured her entrance into the wedding via the deejay gig, Debbie's next step was to choose the perfect playlist. She needed to choose the songs very carefully to subconsciously awaken Auden into realizing that he had made the wrong choice in Ella. She would submit a sample playlist to Mrs. Woods well before the wedding and tell her to have Auden play it over and over again. A few Taylor Swift and Adele songs came to mind, so she jotted them down.

It may be no surprise that the subtlety of song lyrics on the wedding playlist carefully compiled by Debbie completely escaped Auden's notice. He listened to a few songs while he was playing Xbox but was not giving his full concentration to the task. On another occasion he tried to review the songs, but he was too tired from a grapefruit juice cleanse, and so he fell asleep after the first song. He did not try again. Why should he? His mother was an intelligent person and the deejay was a professional. Besides, listening to several hours of wedding reception music and tweaking the playlist would have been a hard thing to do and he was not fond of doing hard things.

At the same time that Debbie secured an entrance to her old boyfriend's wedding, across the state in Palm Beach, a local chatelaine was hosting a dinner party. At her large house overlooking the Atlantic, several of Palm Beach's upper crust gathered in honor of an award-winning poet.

A few days before the party, the hostess was patting herself on the back for securing such a distinguished guest. She told her husband that she was sure her soiree would make the society news.

Her husband asked, "I have never heard of this poet. Where did she come from?"

She replied, "Well of course you would not know of her. You don't exactly run across poets in your line of business, do you? There are not many poets running around factories talking to business owners. I don't know exactly where she comes from, probably from the halls of academia. Of course, she travels the world and meets all sorts of interesting people. She has also won numerous awards for her work."

The husband, who was skeptical by nature, asked, "How do you know that?"

She answered impatiently, "She told me so. That is how I know. Of course, she was very modest about it, but I drew it out in conversation. It is so refreshing to be in the presence of creative, brilliant people. They are so humble and yet such mysterious geniuses. You never know what they are going to do. That is what makes them such interesting dinner guests."

The husband, who did not share his wife's appreciation for mysterious geniuses, rolled his eyes. His wife was in the habit of inviting creative brilliant people to stay in the guesthouse behind their home. They usually ate all his food and borrowed money constantly. His wife called it being a patron of the arts, but he called it supporting freeloaders. However, he loved his wife and was happy to support her interests.

The distinguished poet did not disappoint. The hostess was thrilled at the interesting conversation involving esoteric ideas and faraway places. In reality, none of the guests understood a thing that the poet said but none were willing to admit it. They nodded and feigned understanding. To them, it did not matter if they understood. What mattered was that they had a seat at the table of one of the summer's most prestigious events with one of the area's most influential hostesses. The dinner party was a success, and everyone left late that evening with impressive names to drop and little bits of society gossip to enrich their lives.

Unfortunately, one of the many people gathered at the mansion that day also left with over half a million dollars' worth of the hostess's jewelry tucked into their pockets. The criminal was not apprehended, and the jewelry was never recovered. Similar jewelry heists occurred throughout the summer, mainly at high profile society gatherings. The thieves' pattern of targeting society functions had earned them the moniker "the Silver Spoon Gang."

Local police, FBI agents, and insurance company representatives were both frustrated and baffled at the lack of clues. They did not know if the gang was seasonal like many of the residents or if they were still in Palm Beach hiding in plain sight. All agencies were determined to catch the thieves, so they imported the best and brightest talent to the area. Their common goal was to prevent the next crime and capture the gang.

– Three –
Heavy Weather

THE INDIRECT LIGHT OF THE AFTERNOON SUN shone through the French doors of the elaborately appointed hotel suite. Through the floor-to-ceiling windows of the oceanfront room, one could see the blue green waters of the Atlantic producing a steady surf that broke on the light sand beach. A gentle breeze blew the palm trees that surrounded the expansive grounds of the resort. This picture-perfect scene suddenly became a little darkened as a large gray cloud, probably holding an afternoon rainstorm, floated inland.

There was also a storm brewing inside the white marble bathroom of the suite. It took the form of a very stylish, very petite girl with short blonde hair named Ella Birnam. The overwrought bride-to-be was determined that, though her parents had gone to considerable expense for her elaborate fairytale wedding in Palm Beach, she would under no circumstances marry Auden Woods in three days. The offense was too severe, and she could see no way of bridging the great divide that now separated them. The betrayal was too deep and the revelation of this lying Auden, this phony Auden, this imposter lurking beneath the surface of their eighteen-month relationship was so disturbing that calling off the wedding was the only option she could see.

Deidre, Lady, and Alexandra stood huddled outside the bathroom door as the mother pleaded with her daughter once again, "Tell me sweetie, why are you so upset with Auden? Your aunts are here and we want to help you. Your cousin Alexandra is here too. Please come out."

"Mother, leave me alone!" said Ella, dismissing her mother.

"That's good!" Deidre said. "Don't hold it in, let all your feelings out and we can make some progress. Be authentic. Be yourself. Don't pretend for us."

Deidre was sure that feeding her daughter positive statements would unlock the doors of communication and hopefully unlock the bathroom door in the process. She wanted to harness this negative energy in the room and push it out into a more positive direction. This was her usual method of dealing with her highly sensitive and emotional daughter. The apple had not fallen far from the tree. Of artistic temperament herself, Deidre prided herself on her intuitive insight into the emotional energy that flowed all around her.

Not taking her mother's keen emotional insights seriously, Ella clinched her fists and shouted through the door, "I am not marrying Auden!"

The delegation went to the sitting room to regroup and strategize. Deidre was overwhelmed by feelings of helplessness. She turned to her family. "I don't know what to do. She won't talk to me. All she says is that she won't marry Auden."

Frances said, "Something must have happened to upset her. You know how Ella has to feel all her feelings before she can make sense of anything. I know you are worried, but I think we will have to be patient and wait. She will come out soon."

Alexandra became curious. She had some vague memories of her cousin, mostly fuzzy images or short scenes from childhood. What was Ella like now? Her stepmother never talked about the Fridays, and her father never shared any information about his family. She wanted to know more about her cousin's story. She asked, "How did Ella meet Auden?"

Frances walked toward the bathroom door and answered Alexandra's question with a loud voice, hoping to jog Ella's memory. "It is such a romantic story. Ella and Auden fell in love in South America. They traveled throughout the region to study the coffee culture for their anthropology junior project. Spending so much time together working on a common goal, they discovered that they had so much in common. Ella told me that it was so romantic being together in the tropical jungle away from everything familiar. The steamy climate and the exotic coffee flavors worked like magic and they fell in love."

Lady chimed in with her opinion. "I think Auden fell in love with Ella when he came to the family beach house at Christmas break."

Frances scowled at Lady with a "you're not helping"

look. Lady, as she often did, called the situation the right way. Auden knew that Ella was the girl he could spend the rest of his life with when he met Ella's family on Christmas break. Elizabeth Bennett confessed to her sister Jane in Pride and Prejudice that her love for Mr. Darcy "has been coming on so gradually, that I hardly know when it began. But I believe I must date it from my first seeing his beautiful grounds at Pemberley." So Auden Woods would date his decision to ask for Ella's hand in marriage upon seeing the beautiful Friday family beach house.

Deidre paced back and forth and then plopped down on the couch. She had a pitiful, exhausted look on her face. "What are we going to do?" she repeated.

Frances's phone chimed and she read a text from her eldest daughter. She exhaled and said, "I think I know what the problem is." She held up her phone. "Farryn asked me why Auden hired his old girlfriend to be the wedding deejay?"

As Ella sat in seclusion and scrolled on her new, shiny phone, she questioned her relationship with Auden and their impending marriage. She took pride in her broad, wide, accepting view of everyone and everything, but this was too much. The fact remained: Auden hired his old girlfriend as the wedding deejay and did not tell her. He never mentioned dating a girl named Debbie, and yet their relationship was well documented on social media. And his old girlfriend seemed intent on causing problems. She wondered if, in some situations like this, a little intolerance was a good idea.

Auden's text stating that hiring Debbie was "no big deal" had thrown her into an emotional fury. She was mad at herself for being in the dark and not seeing through him. She now saw her fiancé in a different light. Behind those skinny jeans and that elongated mustache was a chauvinistic, philandering so-and-so. How could she possibly go through with it?

She put her phone down and began looking for things to throw to appease her wrath. She tried throwing the French soaps, but they only made a kind of thudding sound when they hit the wall. The complimentary valet kit made an even less impressive sound hitting the mirror. The bathroom was festooned with plush white towels, but they were of no use in pitching a hissy fit. She was disappointed that this luxury resort did not have glass cups in the bath. She did not know that her mother had swept the room and removed all breakable objects.

Having no available projectiles to use, she sat down on the marble tub and stared at herself in the large mirror. She was one of those girls who wear short hair well. Her small heart-shaped face was accentuated by a stylish haircut with wispy bangs in front. She changed her hair color alternately from dark brown to blonde, depending on her moods. For the wedding it was a platinum blonde color to go with her wedding dress and to blend with her custom headpiece. Even though she was furious and confused and her life was falling apart, she had to admit that she looked good in the bathroom lighting.

Frances pulled up a few social media posts on her phone and showed the others the extent of the problem. "It looks like Debbie Stewart has devised a well-timed social media campaign to win Auden back. She must have posted every picture she had with Auden through the years. And look at these audacious hashtags."

Lady said, "This girl is crazy. Why would Auden hire his old girlfriend to be the deejay?" She gasped as she read the hashtags aloud, "#Seemslikeoldtimes, #goingtomybestfriendswedding, and #heisnotmarriedyet."

Alexandra said, "Look at the last one: #youbelongtome. That's bold."

Lady, who never thought much of Auden's character, said, "Maybe we should look at this as blessing in disguise. I never knew what Ella saw in that boy anyway. She can still get out of it. We will all support her decision."

"We can't call off the wedding!" said Deidre with panic in her voice. "We have spent so much money and done so much planning and all the guests will be upset. It will make us look like fools."

Looking at her sister incredulously, Lady said, "Deidre, who cares what the guests think?"

Frances said, "Lady is right. Ella's happiness is all that matters. Besides, the guests are staying at a world-class resort for the weekend at a phenomenal group rate that I negotiated with the hotel. They should be ecstatic, whether there is a wedding or not."

"You're right," said Deidre. "Of course ... of course, Ella's happiness is all that matters. But, isn't there a way for her to be happy and not cancel the wedding? Auden has so many good qualities. I am sure they can work this out."

"Good qualities? Such as?" said Lady. She continued enumerating what she thought belonged on the liability side of Auden's balance sheet. "He barely graduated with a major in anthropology. He does not have a job or any job prospects. He is wearing sweatpants and tee shirts every time I see him. He has a ridiculous mustache that looks like a walrus. And now this boy genius hires his high school girlfriend for his wedding. I think Ella could do much better. What happed to that guy she dated? What was his name, Bobby? He was a very ambitious young man and he treated her well."

Deidre responded, "Bobby was very nice but his last name was Vader. Ella did not want to go through life with the name Ella Vader. I don't blame her one bit. People would make fun of her every time she said her name. You know that with her sensitive nature she can't take ridicule."

Deidre did not want to come out and say it, but she was not sure that Ella could do better than Auden. She loved her daughter very much, but she could be exhausting at times and, if the truth were known, she was glad to be handing off a majority of the responsibility to Auden.

She continued to defend him. "You're just being judgy again, Lady. Auden is actively looking for a job. He wants a job that he loves going to every day—something that uses all his talents and does not feel like work. I totally support him and admire him for not taking just any job. It takes courage to do what he is doing and they tell me that it may take months or even years to find a fulfilling job."

Providence in its wisdom often puts siblings with opposite personalities in the same family. Who can say that this is not to teach understanding and tolerance? Deidre often made statements that invited argument by a logical person. This time Lady did not argue with her sister. Instead, she said, "I'm sorry, I can't help it. You know I want what is best for Ella and I don't want her to end up with an underachiever."

Deidre pointed her finger at her younger sister and said, "I know Auden is not your cup of tea but remember what you promised? Don't bring out those 'A' words this weekend when you talk about Auden."

Lady nodded that she remembered her promise, although she was thinking of the perfect 'A' word at the moment to describe Auden. She assured her sister, "Don't worry, I will be a saint this weekend. You will hear only good words and happy thoughts from me."

Alexandra wondered what they were talking about and asked, "What are the 'A' words?"

Deidre explained. "Words like ambition, achievement, accomplishment, upset Ella and Auden. They don't like to be measured or evaluated or compared to other people's accomplishments."

Frances had listened to Lady and Deidre interact for over twenty years. Usually, it was entertaining to watch two sisters with opposite personalities try to understand each other, but today it was getting them nowhere. They needed a solution and they needed it fast. She knew that Ella was probably getting hungry and could not resist sushi. She suggested, "Let's order room service." Much like opening a can of tuna to get a cat out of a tree, she planned to lure her niece out of the bathroom with raw fish.

Nothing restores the body and gives clarity to the mind like a good meal. The room service attendant rolled a heavily laden cart into the suite. Even though they were in a family crisis, all the women smiled as they surveyed the display of delicious food. They had ordered a variety of items, including an assortment of sushi. Alexandra ordered the turkey and bacon club with crispy fries which the Breakers is known for. Lady, of course, added tea and scones to the order.

Frances, speaking to the bathroom door, said, "Ella, it's Aunt Frances. We ordered your favorite sushi."

Ella was receptive to her Aunt Frances. She liked talking to her about her life. She asked good questions like, "How did that make you feel?" or "What did you do when that happened?" or "What do you want to do?" She would not judge her and say things like "Why did you do that?" or "What were you thinking?" like her parents were apt to say. She trusted her aunt, and she was getting hungry, so she turned the door latch and walked out into the spacious sitting room. As she hugged her aunt, she forced a smile, turned to her cousin and said, "Hello, Alexandra, it is good to see you again."

Ella sat down, nibbled on sushi, and poured out her feelings. As she finished a tuna roll, she said, "I don't think I can marry Auden. I don't trust him anymore. He is already morphing into a person I don't know. He has been pretending to have a broad and flexible outlook on life but really he is a narrow-minded, two-timing chauvinist."

Deidre looked thoughtful but said nothing. She did not want to excite her daughter in the direction of calling off the wedding. Lady did not know what to say because she would have never gotten into this situation. Alexandra had barely dated in high school and she told herself she had nothing to add to the conversation about relationships. They all instinctively turned towards Frances.

Frances was also thinking. She was thinking of her wedding day and trying to remember her feelings. Although Frances was very different from Ella, she tried to put herself in Ella's shoes. Marriage was a huge commitment, and Ella was right to stop and think through this situation. She said to her niece, "I know you are very upset and feel betrayed. Auden should have told you about his relationship with Debbie. And his mother should not have hired her for the wedding. They made a big mistake."

All four women nodded in agreement, especially Lady. Frances continued. "Every relationship has its challenges. You know your marriage will be filled with situations like this where there will have to be communication, understanding and especially forgiveness." Pointing to Deidre she continued, "Your marriage will be like one of your mother's beautifully blown glass vases that are put into the fire only to come out more beautiful."

Deidre was very pleased that Frances referred to her glass-blowing art. She spent a good amount of time in the hot shop expressing her creativity in this art form. She was proud of her artistic talents, as it was the only thing that she thought made her special. Her warm glow from the compliment quickly turned to panic when Frances added, "You have to decide if you want to spend the rest of your life with Auden working through the challenges of marriage together. I'm sure we will all be behind you if you decide you don't want to go through with it."

"Ella, what made you want to marry him?" asked Lady with emphasis on the word "him." "Can you remember what attracted you in the first place? Why Auden Woods?"

Ella reminisced and said in a wispy voice. "I remember the first time I knew. I looked across the South American coffee shop and watched him playing the ukulele and singing 'I'm Yours.' I thought, 'This is a guy I could hang out with for a long time.' I really do adore him even though he can be a stupid poop."

Frances asked, "Have you spoken with Auden to hear his side of the story?"

"Did he say he was sorry for hiring his old girlfriend? Did he say why he let that happen?" asked Lady.

"He did not actually say he was sorry. He just texted that it was no big deal and that his mom is the one who hired the deejay." Ella held out the phone so they could read his recent text.

"Well, based on his text, it looks like he did not know Debbie's intentions to try and come between you," said Frances.

Lady was astounded at how easily they were letting this guy off the hook. In her mind, a real man would have driven to Palm Beach, all night if necessary, to speak to his troubled bride in person, reassuring her of his love and devotion. "How can you know his intentions from ten words in a text? Did he call you or try to apologize in any other way?"

Ignoring Lady's comment, Frances continued, "Can you think of a way you can forgive him and move forward? Is there anything he can do to regain your trust?"

Ella considered. "I think he should show his love for me by firing the deejay, making his mom apologize to me for hiring his old girlfriend, and buying me some jewelry."

"Okay, one thing at a time. Let's start with firing the old girlfriend-deejay," said Frances. "Why don't you talk to him and tell him that is what you want."

Frances knew getting Auden's mom to apologize to her future daughter-in-law was a project on the scale of brokering peace in the Middle East. That was tomorrow's problem. The jewelry could come later too. Ella texted Auden. Auden was a reasonable young man, and since he was not paying for any of the wedding, he was able to quickly agree to her request. Auden texted Ella.

"He talked with his mom and she said if we fire Debbie we have to hire another deejay," Ella said with delight. "He says he does not really care and we can do whatever we want. And, how sweet, he says, 'Whatever makes you happy' and he used a double heart emoji." She showed the text to her aunts and cousin. "He never uses heart emojis so I can tell he is really sorry and really loves me." Ella hugged her phone to her chest and giggled. If she had been wearing a mood ring the color would have changed from black to bright blue within thirty seconds.

Despite being recently well fed from room service, Deidre was feeling faint. She was overjoyed that Frances had talked her high-strung daughter down off the pre-marital ledge, but now they had to find a wedding deejay at the last minute. Lady read her sister's mind. She asked, "Who is going to call Debbie and fire her. Someone should also talk to Auden's mom? And, where on earth are we going to find a deejay at this late hour?"

Ella said, "Well I'm not talking to Debbie Stewart or Auden's mom!"

Deidre said, "I don't want to talk to them either. I don't have the energy for such an unpleasant conversation."

Lady said, "I don't want to do it either. I might say what I really think and then regret it later."

Frances wondered if she should offer to make the call

for them. She liked to help people, especially her family, but was this her job to do? She had already talked Ella through her doubts about marriage. Did she have to handle this deejay situation too? Her husband would remind her that sometimes she went too far and got too involved. Was this going to be one of those times? She had just told Thomas in the lobby that families must stick together and help each other no matter what. Did she really believe that?

Frances decided. "I will talk to Auden's mom and tell her to fire Debbie. I may have to bargain with her. She is a shrewd woman and will probably want something in return. Also, I know a guy in Fort Lauderdale who is an experienced deejay. Lady, Alexandra, and I will go see him first thing tomorrow."

– Four –
Back On Again

ELLA'S TALK WITH HER AUNT FRANCES combined with Auden's heartfelt text pulled her out of her emotional funk. She grabbed Alexandra's hand and said, "Come on, cousin. I want to show you my dress." Ella pulled her off the couch and dragged her down the hallway into the bedroom. The bride's wedding ensemble was laid out all over the room like a museum display. Alexandra had not thought much about wedding dresses and was not really into fashion but was speechless at the beautiful things arranged around the room. Ella's gown was the most beautiful dress she had ever seen, and she said so.

Ella twirled around and held out her arm with a long necklace draped across it. "I'm going to wear the family pearls. Grandpa Friday bought these for Grandma right here in Palm Beach over fifty years ago," Ella said, proudly displaying the very impressive family heirloom. "And these are the matching earrings and bracelets. And here is my headpiece. I designed it and Mommy had it custom made." She handed it to Alexandra.

Alexandra handled the headpiece reverently, admiring the beautiful craftsmanship incorporating pearls and crystals on the pink velvet band. "It's so pretty," she said. "It looks like something out of the Gatsby movie."

Ella squealed and slipped it on her head. Alexandra stared admiringly at her cousin. "You even look like Daisy from the movie."

Ella was thrilled at this comparison. Although she had just renewed her relationship with her cousin, she could tell that Alexandra was not the type of person to hand out empty flattery. Ella had a sixth sense about people. Her teachers had labored trying to get her to read literature and comprehend science, but they did not have to teach her how to read people.

Frances watched the girls from the sitting room. She was pleased that Ella had so quickly renewed her friendship with Alexandra. It was as if they picked up where they left off ten years ago. She had a flashback of the two girls wearing princess dresses at Disney World getting Cinderella's autograph. Overhearing the words "heirloom pearls" she said, "Deidre, you should put those pearls in the hotel safe until the wedding. I would not leave them lying around. You should also probably have someone in charge of them at the wedding. Especially when Ella changes dresses for the reception."

"Oh, Frances," said Deidre. "You are so suspicious. No one is going to come to the wedding and steal our jewelry. All the people coming to our wedding are good people."

"I'm just saying it would be a good idea," said Frances. "In all the confusion, someone may walk off with them." Deidre waved her hand at her and so she dropped the subject.

Walking back into the sitting room Ella said, "Mommy, Alexandra has to come to my bachelorette party." Ella turned to her Aunt Frances and said, "Aunt Franny, I don't know what to do for my bachelorette party. All the bridesmaids will arrive tomorrow and I can't decide what to do. I want it to be fun and I want people to talk about it and post pictures the whole time. What should I do?"

Lady looked at Deidre and said in an alarmed voice, "You have not planned the bachelorette party yet? Isn't that the maid of honor's job? Isn't it a little late to plan a party?"

Deidre responded, "We were so busy planning every-thing else that we didn't get around to it. Ella doesn't really have a maid of honor. She says all her friends are special and deserve equal honor. You know Ella, she has to do things her own way—not the traditional way."

Frances asked Ella, "What do you want to do? What do you like to do with your friends when you have free time?"

"Honestly, I just like to hang," said Ella. "I read all the bride's magazines and it looks like I should have some sort of wild party with a male stripper."

Deidre added, "Yes, all the magazines and social media have pictures of girls drinking excessively and cheering on a muscular man in a bikini." A thought occurred to Deidre and she snapped her fingers. "I know, maybe we could call Reggie Watson, Ella's old school friend. I remember Reggie in first grade. He always took off his uniform on the playground during recess. Maybe he still has leanings in that direction. We have to make sure we do what other people want to do."

Lady said, "It doesn't matter what other people want to do. This party is about Ella and what Ella wants to do."

Ella admitted, "I don't really want to get drunk. I don't want my bridesmaids drunk either. At my friend Shanna's morning wedding, all the bridesmaids looked awful in the pictures because they got totally wasted at the bachelorette party the night before."

Deidre reassured her, "Ella, honey, your friends won't get drunk. They're nice girls."

Ella thought about each bridesmaid. She said, "I guess you are right, although I'm worried about one of my bridesmaids. My friend Brandy has never been to Florida and she might go all spring break this weekend."

"What do you mean by 'going all spring break,'" questioned Lady.

"You know, go crazy and be out of control," said Ella.

Frances clarified the term for Lady. "What she means is that normally intelligent young women sometimes become unpredictable versions of themselves when they hit the tropical climate for the first time. This transformation is of course aggravated by alcohol."

Ella thought about her party for a few moments. Not taxing her brain too much, she finally said, "I don't want to have a lame party, but I just want to hang with my friends by the pool and take some pictures on the beach."

"Then that is what you will do," said Frances decisively.

"I'll call my friend who works at the hotel and reserve a poolside bungalow and order food for the party."

Ella was relieved and was now actually looking forward to her bachelorette party. Her creative ideas started to flow. "We need music," she said. "Aunt Frances, can you ask your deejay friend if they can come tomorrow night and deejay the bachelorette party also?"

"I'm sure it won't be a problem," said Frances reassuringly, although she was not really sure. She hoped that deejay would remember her and would be willing to come at the last minute.

As she closed the door to the suite and walked down the hallway with Lady and Alexandra, Frances felt happy. In a few hours they had worked together, and the wedding was back on again. The bride and her mother had been restored to a joyful, expectant state. She smiled, thinking that this is what families do for each other. It made her feel useful and it made her feel good. She voiced her thoughts. "That turned out well."

Back in her room, she called Auden's mother to sort out how to fire the old girlfriend deejay. The mother of the groom was uncooperative at first and complained about the last minute cancellation. To smooth things over with Ella's future in-laws, Frances took the liberty of making a deal with the groom's mother. It was a deal that Frances hoped would not upset Deidre and Ella. She was a little worried how it would all turn out. She told herself today's problem was solved, and she should really be happy. She would worry about tomorrow's problems tomorrow.

While the mood swung from distress to relief in the suite, Thomas found himself in a content and happy mood. For one thing, he liked staying at this resort because of the attention they gave to the outdoor landscape as well as the indoor foliage. Also, he was relieved that his sisters did not ask him to accompany them and help sort out wedding drama. And finally, he was happy because a book that he ordered arrived on his doorstep just before he departed from Sarasota to make the drive to Palm Beach.

Thomas's hobby, or one could argue his obsession, was gardening. He specifically liked learning about native Florida plants. He packed his new book, *The Expert's Guide to Florida Orchids*, by renowned University of Florida professor Stanley Martin. He found a comfortable chair in a quiet spot in the loggia, opened his book, began to read, and in a short time fell into a peaceful nap.

Thomas awoke from his nap with a start when he heard a person behind him yell, "Ouch!" Thomas had been dreaming a recurrent dream about sport fishing in Boca Grande. In his dream he was tightly grasping a fishing rod and reeling in an enormous tarpon. The tarpon was putting up a brave fight and Thomas was pulling and yanking back on the line. In reality, he was waving his book over his head and finally catapulted it in the air, hitting an innocent hotel guest behind him.

He quickly got up from his chair and turned around

to see the victim of his book hurtling. He saw a full-figured woman dressed in a long flowing kaftan of tropical print. She was wearing colorful earrings that dangled back and forth and a matching necklace that looked like it weighed twenty pounds. Her unnaturally uniform strawberry blonde hair seemed to move back and forth like a wig as she rubbed the sore spot on her head. Thomas thought to himself that she smelled strongly of gardenias.

"I am so sorry. I was catching a tarpon. I mean, I mean I was dreaming. Are you all right?"

The woman picked up Thomas's book and, reading the cover, said, "I am quite all right. I see you are a fan of Stanley Martin. I am also a fellow orchid lover. My name is Angela Beaumonde. You have probably heard of me."

Thomas admitted, "No, I have not but it's nice to meet you." Coming from behind his chair and extending his hand he added, "I'm Thomas Friday. I'm glad to meet a fellow orchid lover. Aren't the flowers in this hotel exquisite?"

"You took the words out of my mouth," said Angela extending her hand high in the air as if she wanted Thomas to kiss it. "What brings you to Palm Beach?"

Thomas did not kiss her hand but shook it at eye level and explained, "I'm here for my niece's wedding on Saturday. What brings you here, Angela?"

"I am here for the Gem and Jewelry Exhibition. One of my pieces is expected to win first prize. You see," she said, displaying her necklace and earrings, "I am a well-known, international jewelry designer."

"That sounds impressive. I've never met an international jewelry designer," said Thomas admiringly. He wondered what caused a person to jump from the national to international level in jewelry design.

"You should come to the show and buy a few pieces for your wife."

"I don't have a wife. Well I did. I had two actually. I mean not at the same time. I had, uh one at a time," said Thomas, fumbling trying to make his meaning clear. Going with the jewelry theme, he said, "My niece loves jewelry. Can't get enough of the stuff. She is going to load up with her grandmother's heirloom pearls for her wedding this weekend. There must be hundreds of pearls between the necklace, earrings, and what are those things you wear on your arm?"

"Bracelets," said Angela.

"Yes, bracelets. I don't know how she is going to move with all that jewelry. And my daughter Alexandra wants to wear her late mother's diamond necklace. It is so heavy. I bet her neck is going to ache and I predict that she will probably take it off before the end of the night. And my sister Lady, you should see the sapphire and diamond ring she totes around on these special occasions. She says it is just like the one Princess Diana wore. I have to tell you that I don't understand a woman's fascination with jewelry."

"Jewelry is fascinating, isn't it," said Angela. "How interesting that your family has such valuable heirloom diamonds and pearls. And you say the wedding is here on Saturday night?"

"No, the wedding is at the Flagler Museum," corrected Thomas.

"How interesting." Angela seemed to be concentrating on something and then wrapped up the meeting quickly by saying, "Well, Thomas, it was nice to meet you. I have to run."

Thomas was surprised by her sudden departure. He called after her, "I hope we will meet again, Angela."

She turned and called to him over her shoulder, "Somehow, I think we will meet again. Goodbye, Thomas."

– Five –
The Unusual Replacement

FRANCES WAS LOOKING AT HER WATCH and regretting her decision to take the scenic route to Fort Lauderdale. The seasonal traffic made their progress slower than she expected. As they sat in traffic, she looked out the window. Florida, as she often does, had provided another beautiful day. The sun was shining. The cool ocean breeze was gently blowing, and the sea birds swooped and circled over the water. The traffic started to move and they made their way south on Ocean Boulevard, passing palm-tree-lined streets on the right and the Worth Avenue clock tower standing watch over the blue-green waters of the Atlantic Ocean on the left.

Lady said, "I hope we can make it there and back before lunch. The sooner we can get a deejay the sooner we can relieve Deidre's anxiety."

Alexandra did not mind the delay. She was experiencing an unusual feeling of contentment and even happiness. She could not put her finger on the source of her sublime feelings. Was it the beautiful tropical scenery of this place compared to the cold gray Northeast she was accustomed to at school? Was it the happy occasion of a wedding with her recently restored family? Was it the relief of not having to placate her emotional stepmother on her school breaks? She was not sure of the reason, but she liked the feeling.

As they headed south, she put her head back on the car headrest, looked at the clear blue sky through the sunroof, and was thankful she was on this little adventure to save her cousin's wedding. She was quiet and listened to the conversation in the front seat intermittently with her own thoughts. She was content to be with two women that seemed to care about her greatly although they had not spent time with her in years. She would have to figure out the source of these peaceful, happy feelings another time. They had arrived at their destination.

Frances parked in front of a colorful bungalow. She turned to Alexandra and Lady and said, "There is something I should probably tell you about Dylan. He is kind of … Well, he used to be … I mean he sometimes …" Dylan Thompson defied a quick description, so she said, "Never mind, come on, you'll see."

After ringing the doorbell, they stood for some time on the wide porch admiring the Arts and Crafts elements of Dylan's home.

Lady commented, "I love these old bungalows, although these colors are a bit loud for my taste."

"I like these colors," said Alexandra. "It looks like an artist lives here."

Frances thought how much this house restoration mirrored Dylan's life and commented, "Yes, he is really giving new life to this rundown house."

"Look at all that wood piled up in the yard," Alexandra noticed.

"That is probably from the hurricane," Lady informed her. "The last hurricane left so much debris, people are still dealing with it."

"It does not look like all those trees have come from this yard," observed Frances. "I think Dylan has gone around the neighborhood and collected the wood and is going to make things out of it. You were right, Alexandra; this is an artist's bungalow. Dylan is not only a musician but he also makes beautiful pieces out of recycled wood."

A man popped around the corner of the house and shouted, "Who can it be now?"

Dylan Thompson was a slim man of average height in his late thirties. He looked older and more worn than he should, owing to years of abusing his body with alcohol and drugs. He had shoulder-length shaggy brown hair, an earring in one ear, and an assortment of tattoos on his body. Lady was secretly thinking to herself and repeating in her mind, "Don't judge a book by its cover. Don't judge a book by its cover." Everyone knows the truth behind this moral axiom, but few follow it and Lady was no exception. She eased her mind by remembering "Frances knows what she is doing."

Very different thoughts filled Alexandra's head. She thought Dylan had a cool guy vibe despite his worn-looking appearance. Like fashionable designer jeans that are actually better when they are ripped and faded and torn, she thought Dylan looked like the perfect wedding deejay. She was confident that Ella and Auden would like him too.

Walking closer and taking off his gardening gloves, he immediately recognized Frances and shouted, "Is it just my imagination or is that Franny Friday? Heaven must be missing an angel."

"Hello, Dylan," said Frances. "Please excuse our barging in on you like this. It looks like we interrupted your gardening. I tried to call but I think I have an old number."

"Did you dial 867-5309?" asked Dylan.

"Yes," answered Frances, confused. "There was no answer. It just kept ringing."

"It's the telephone line," he said explaining the difficulty with his cell phone. "That's just the way it is. I would complain but I don't want to rock the boat. Luckily, I heard you knock three times." Opening the front door for them, he said, "Walk this way."

He led the three women into the living room of the historic bungalow. The skilled homeowner was carefully restoring his 1920s home to its original beauty. He had uncovered and refinished the built-in bookcases and behind a drywall façade he found beautiful decorative tiles surrounding the fireplace. Gustav Stickley, the man who brought the Arts and Crafts movement to this country, would have approved of the care and attention he was giving to this restoration.

After introductions, Frances said, "Dylan, it is so good to see you looking so well and this house is coming along beautifully."

"Well, Franny, since I turned the beat around, I'm on top of the world. I can't always get what I want. Still, I have survived. I've only just begun on this house renovation but it is coming along day by day. I have to say that I am becoming a pretty good handyman."

"You sure are," said Frances warmly. "When did we first meet? How long ago was that?"

"I think it was 1999—when we were young," he answered.

Looking at Lady and Alexandra, he added, "Before I met Frances my life was just wasted days and wasted nights. I just needed someone to show me the way."

Looking at her watch and knowing time was short, Frances got right to the purpose of their visit. "Dylan, we've got a problem we hope you can help us with. My niece is going to be married this weekend and we need a deejay for the wedding and the bachelorette party. We had a deejay but, well, it didn't work out. It's a long story. Can you help?"

Dylan looked at Alexandra and smiled a charming smile. "So you are going to the chapel and you're going to get married?"

"No! No! I am not getting married," said Alexandra with too much determination in her voice. "My cousin Ella is the bride."

"I see. You will be a single lady at the wedding. Are you ever gonna fall in love again?" said Dylan teasing her.

"No! I don't even have a boyfriend," said Alexandra. She felt she should explain. "I had a boyfriend my senior year but we broke up. Actually he broke up with me and embarrassed me in front of the whole school, but that is a really long story and not really important right now."

She wondered why she was giving so much information to a man she had just met.

Dylan sympathized with her. "Breaking up is hard to do. You should have told him, 'Don't do me like that.' Still, looks like you are over it. I hope there is no bad blood."

Dylan stopped questioning Alexandra and in his mind he drifted into a reverie of a girl he used to love but gave up for his rock band. He often thought of her and what might have been. He thought to himself, "She's out of my life. It's too late to turn back now." Realizing he was daydreaming he came back to the conversation and added, "I'm sorry. I was in a daydream. It's a hard habit to break."

Frances said firmly, "Dylan, I need you to focus." Handing him a sheet of paper she said, "Can you pull together this playlist and be at the Flagler Museum on Saturday? Also, we need you for the bachelorette party at The Breakers tonight. You will be well fed and well paid. And, we would love for you to be a part of our family's special celebration."

Dylan took the paper and said, "Thank you for the music." Then he swiped left and right on his phone as he squinted to see his calendar. He said in a frustrated tone, "I still haven't found what I'm looking for. These eyes!" He exited the living room in search of his reading glasses.

As he left the room, Lady leaned over to the others and whispered, "I don't know if this is a good idea. Dylan seems really odd and he speaks in weird phrases."

Alexandra whispered back, "I picked up on a few song titles but I thought he was just being funny."

Frances defended her friend. "Dylan is a musical genius and has a nearly photographic memory. His brain can retain thousands of songs. That is what makes him such good deejay. I thought you would probably notice his quirky way of talking."

"Notice! How can we not notice, Frances? He is a walking talking jukebox," whispered Lady excitedly. "Can you ask him to speak normal, at least during the wedding?"

"He can't," said Frances. "He does not realize he is doing it and he is not trying to be funny. It is especially noticeable when he meets new people or is nervous about something."

Lady was not assured. She said warily, "I can just see the look on Deidre and Ella's faces when they meet him. We will never hear the end of it if this goes south. At family reunions I can just hear them telling everyone, 'Remember the oddball deejay that Frances and Lady scrounged up for Ella's wedding.'"

"Don't write him off, Lady!" said Frances sternly but still in a whisper. "He has turned his life around and has more potential than you can imagine. There are worse afflictions than over-quoting song titles. I have complete faith in Dylan. You will see."

Alexandra held her phone up to show her two aunts. "I just looked him up on the Rate Your Deejay site and he has a 4.5/5 rating. The only negative reviews are from people who did not like his tattoos and shaggy hair. Otherwise the feedback is all good."

An uneasy feeling crept over Lady as she watched Dylan searching haphazardly for his glasses in the other room. She made a decision not to worry and to trust her sister-in-law's judgment.

Dylan entered the room with his spectacles and said, "I'll be there. Don't you worry about a thing."

"Fantastic!" said Frances. She breathed an audible sigh of relief. She had been holding her breath since the moment she volunteered to find a deejay. She knew that Dylan was a sought after professional and she told herself that this was nothing short of a miracle that he was available this weekend. She started to get up, thinking their errand was complete, when she noticed Dylan sit down in his well-worn leather chair.

He folded his hands, closed his eyes, took a deep breath and said, "Now tell me about the bride and groom so I can get their vibe. It's got to be real. If they were here I would ask them 'Who are you?' Hit me with your best shot. Tell me something good."

Lady said, "Ella and Auden were very careful to pick out the new songs for the wedding after they fired the old deejay. I think we should at least start with those songs, especially since we are short on time."

Dylan ignored Lady's comment and kept his eyes closed. He felt like saying to her 'Have you never been mellow?' but he did not. He realized that people who were sticklers about details often questioned his method of delivering deejay services.

Frances sat back down on the sofa and filled Dylan in on the wedding couple. She had no trouble describing her niece Ella, but she did have trouble trying to describe Auden. She said his most defining quality seemed to be that he was very popular among his friends. She also told Dylan about the recent crisis of the old girlfriend being hired and subsequently fired to which he commented, "Wow, the games people play. It must have been hard for her to realize 'I'm not that girl.'" He continued listening with his eyes closed, forming a picture of the wedding couple and matching them with the perfect music.

After Frances finished her narrative, he suddenly opened his eyes. He rose from the chair, ran his hand through his tousled hair and said, "I need to start taking care of business. I had better get the party playlist started." Dylan walked the women to their car as a light rain shower moved over the house. He said, "Raindrops are falling on my head but that's the way I like it. Oh look, here comes the sun."

As Dylan shut the front door of his bungalow, he crumpled up the playlist and made a three-point shot into the trashcan. He walked into his study and got to work on the music for Ella and Auden's wedding. He smiled and said out loud, "I'm going to do it my way."

– Six –
Lunch & Shopping

DRIVING TO FORT LAUDERDALE and securing one of the area's best wedding deejays had given Frances an appetite. She turned off A1A at the coral stone pillars marking Worth Avenue and was lucky enough to see a Maserati pulling out of a parking space in front of Saks Fifth Avenue. She took the space, turned off the car. Referring to the success of their morning's errand she said, "That went well. We have earned a nice lunch. Let's find a café and then do some shopping."

"You mean we will do some window-shopping," said Lady, alluding to the high-end shops that are located along Worth Avenue. "These are the kind of expensive stores where the salespeople practically walk you out to your car with your purchases because you have spent so much money."

"You never know what you will find," said Frances. "Some stores can have great sales." She held up Thomas's platinum credit card. "Anyway, Thomas asked us to take Alexandra and help her pick out a new Florida wardrobe and charge everything to his card. I think we should make Thomas happy and spend some of his money."

"Well in that case, let's get started," Lady said with a devious look in her eyes.

At first, Alexandra felt a little resentment towards her dad for suggesting that she needed a new wardrobe. As if he could wave his credit card and erase his parental mistakes. Besides, what was wrong with her clothes, and why did she need to change anything? As she stepped out of the car into the sunshine her feelings of resentment started to melt away. On the other hand, she was touched by his generous offer. She could not remember many times in her life when her father made such a personal gesture. She decided to take the gift that was offered and enjoy this time with her aunts.

The women strolled up the palm-tree-lined streets filled with high-end shops, art galleries, and restaurants. The Florida sun was shining in the cloudless, bright blue sky. Alexandra stared up at the beautiful lush purple vines climbing up the storefronts and felt the sun on her face. If her father, Thomas, was present, he could have pointed out that the tall trees were coconut palms and the beautiful flowering vines were bougainvillea.

She was still looking sunward when she suddenly felt the sensation of no longer walking, but rather falling forward. It was as if she had tripped over a hidden wire. She caught herself on a nearby palm tree and looked down to find a black and white border collie with its leather leash wrapped around her ankles. The dog was energetically wagging its tail and licking Alexandra's knees, trying to get her attention. A voice from behind her said, "I am so sorry. Stop licking her, Daisy. Are you all right?"

Once she was untangled, Alexandra looked up and saw a young man in shorts, flip-flops, and a polo shirt at the other end of the leash. He was tan and had sandy-colored shoulder-length hair. He was looking down at her with a concerned look. He was looking down because he was at least six inches taller than her. She could not speak at first because she was still recovering from her fall, and because his stunning smile and blue eyes were mesmerizing. She collected herself, bent down, petted the dog, and said, "I'm all right. What a cute dog." Not knowing what else to say to this attractive man, she fled the scene and walked to catch up with her aunts.

They entered a café, where they opted for an outside table. After placing their order, they settled into easy conversation. Frances asked, "Alexandra, what are your plans now that you are a high school graduate? Do you plan to go to college or do you have a job in mind? Are you going to stay in Florida?"

Alexandra was a little embarrassed to give her answer. "I don't really know what is next. I kind of made a mistake with the whole college thing."

"What do you mean?" asked Lady. "How did you make a mistake?"

Alexandra explained. "I was surrounded by such high achievers at my private school. I was so caught up in the frenzy of doing what everyone else was doing that I never took time to think about what I really want to do with my life. I did not get into any of the colleges up north. I was embarrassed so I told my friends I was taking a gap year. I did not tell them that I had no other option."

Frances said, "You should not be embarrassed. People often take a gap year to figure out what they want to do. It may turn out to be a very good thing you did not get into those colleges. There are countless stories of successful people who did not go to college or even dropped out of college to pursue their dreams. You will be just fine."

Lady added, "Besides, who wants to go to school in the freezing cold?"

Alexandra felt affirmed by her aunts. She continued, "I feel like since I have been in Florida, I'm not so stressed about it. I'm actually starting to get excited about my options. I will apply to Florida schools next fall. Until then, I don't really know what I'm going to do—probably get a job."

During a lull in the conversation, Alexandra noticed that the tall guy and his dog had entered the café and taken a seat at an outdoor table not far away.

Frances and Lady also noticed and looked at each other with raised eyebrows.

Lady changed the course of the conversation and returned to the most interesting thing that she had heard Alexandra say in the past two days. She asked, "I don't want to pry but you told Dylan that a boy broke your heart. Do you want to talk about that?"

Alexandra felt completely safe in the company of her two aunts even though she had not seen them in ten years. She opened up and told them the story. "I don't mind talking about it. I dated a guy my senior year. He was my first real boyfriend. I think we were both kind of bored with school and looking for something to do.

He changed from being happy to see me to acting like I annoyed him. He ended our relationship by staging a big breakup scene in front of all our friends and telling another girl he liked her better than me. I think he did it to impress her more than hurt me. Still, it really sucked. I was so happy to graduate and move on."

Lady, who was a defender of women, spoke first. "That does suck! You are better off without him. There are better fish in the sea. He is not even a fish. He is a worm," she added, showing the loyalty that a family member, especially an aunt, can show.

Frances said, "Lady is right. High school is in the past. You have plenty of time to meet guys who will not treat you that way. I think you will look back and see it as a good learning experience."

Now that she had broken the ice with her aunts, Alexandra thought she would ask them a question that had been bothering her for some time. She asked, "Do you think girls really marry men like their father?"

Lady and Frances burst into laughter. Lady said, "Oh, Alexandra, are you worried that you will marry a scatterbrain like your father? Don't worry. I think Thomas broke the mold. There are not many men like him."

Alexandra said, "I know he is intelligent and a very successful businessman but he says such odd things. The other day, I asked him if he had an Allen wrench because I wanted to fix my bicycle. He said he did not know anyone by that name or if they could fix bikes. Then, on the way here, I told him that if I wanted to get a job at the mall, I would have to take a polygraph test. He said he would help me study because he had always been good at math."

Frances laughed, thinking of the many times Thomas Friday misunderstood the situation and how easily he became confused. She said, "Your father is one of the most interesting men I know. Beneath his disheveled, distracted exterior is a heart of gold."

Alexandra's tone saddened. "Sometimes I feel like I hardly know him. He was always working when I was home on school breaks."

Frances said, "I know your father worked a lot when you were younger but now that he is semi-retired, he has more time. It sounds like you will have to get to know him all over again."

Alexandra started to feel like she was dominating the conversation with her problems, so she changed the subject. She asked, "So how did you meet Dylan? He is a very interesting person."

"Sam and I met Dylan in an auto accident. Dylan was driving his car while he was high. He ran a stop sign and smashed into our car. His little sister was in the car with him and she had to be taken to the hospital. We were fine but we followed him to the hospital to see if she was all right. She was fine—just a few stiches. Dylan felt so guilty and upset. He was miserable. Sam gave him his number and told him that he was available if he ever wanted to talk. Sam and Dylan became friends and met together regularly for lunch or coffee. We even met his girlfriend who wanted to move down from up north."

Frances continued, "Dylan decided that he did not

want to move in with his girlfriend so he broke up with her and went on the road with his band. We lost touch with him until he showed up on our doorstep several years later, stoned and needing medical attention. He lived in our rental condo for a few months while he cleaned up. He has been sober ever since."

"Wow, Dylan seems so happy. I would never guess he had such a tough life," said Alexandra.

"He is happy now," said Frances. "He really turned his life around. He will tell you that he never wants to go back to being angry, depressed, and unhappy all the time."

"Did the girlfriend ever take him back?" asked Alexandra.

"No, she was too hurt and did not talk to him again. They may still have a future—you never know."

As the waiter put a grouper sandwich with a side of fries before her, Alexandra commented, "Brittany would faint if she saw me eating this. She used to watch everything I ate and sometimes she ordered for me."

"How did that make you feel?" asked Frances.

"I always felt under pressure to be thin and look a certain way. We argued constantly about the clothes I wore. She wanted me to look like the homecoming queen and I just wanted to be comfortable. We never got along. I think she was just putting up with me. I know they were getting a divorce at the time but she didn't even come to my graduation. I wish it had been different, but don't know what I could have done."

"You couldn't have done anything. None of that

was your fault," said Frances. "Sometimes when people are unhappy with themselves they take it out on others around them, especially kids. I knew Brittany and she probably did not do it intentionally. She was probably unhappy with her own appearance and so projected that on you."

Lady could not agree with Frances's point of view. She was a champion of children who were bullied or picked on by adults. Hearing that Brittany ordered food for a teenage girl appalled her. She exclaimed, "I knew Brittany too. Frances is being too kind. Brittany was a selfish, vain person that would pitch a fit and ruin the party if she did not get things her way. It was ridiculous for her to order your food and selfish of her not to come to your graduation."

"Well, none of us are perfect," said Frances. She decided to change the subject because Lady was prone to tirades about the woman that had hurt her brother. Frances asked, "Alexandra, have you ever met any of your mother's Greek relatives?"

"No, I have never met them. My dad says there are a lot of my mother's family in Tarpon Springs, Florida."

Lady said, "The Greek families have some great restaurants and bakeries in Tarpon Springs."

Frances added, "We will have to take you to meet your Aunt Thea, your mother's sister. She used to help take care of you when you were a baby. I know she would love to reconnect with you."

"I would like that," said Alexandra. She was excited at the prospect of discovering her Greek roots.

The three women finished their lunch and began to wander in and out of shops, making purchases. There are economic principles that can easily be observed and always hold true. There is the management concept called the Peter Principle, which roughly states, "People rise to the level of their incompetence." There is also a time concept called Parkinson's Law that points out the tendency of people to take all the time allotted, and more, to accomplish a task.

There should be an economic principle to describe the phenomenon of human behavior when shopping, especially shopping with other people's money. It has not been given a name yet, but it could be called the "spending other people's money" law. As a result of this principle in action, Frances, Lady, and Alexandra adroitly navigated in and out of more than seventeen boutiques and purchased over twenty items. The total time, including lunch, that it took to assemble Alexandra's Florida wardrobe was only two hours and fifteen minutes. This was possible mainly because the normal hesitation to spend personal, hard-earned money was curiously absent.

The last shop they visited was a boutique specializing in items for the home. Their final task was to find a wedding gift for Ella and Auden as Thomas had requested. As they were browsing, the tall guy and his dog entered the store. He started looking around at various items while his border collie stared at her reflection in an antique mirror. The young man walked over to where Frances and Alexandra were standing and started a conversation. He said, "My friend is having a dinner party and I want to bring a gift for her. I don't want to bring the same old bottle of wine. What would you recommend?"

Frances, wanting more information, said in a cheery voice, "Well that depends on your relationship with the girl. Is she your girlfriend or just a girl who is a friend?"

"Oh, no," he said. "She is not my girlfriend. Just a friend."

Alexandra, being reticent by nature and feeling that the guy was more interested in talking to Aunt Frances than to her, petted the dog and walked toward the back of the store. Frances looked incredulously at Alexandra's back as she walked away. She introduced herself to the young man. "I am Frances Friday, what is your name?"

Very politely, and with a winning smile he answered, "It is nice to meet you, Frances. My name is Brick Davis."

Frances eyed him closely and said, "Hmm. Is Brick Davis your real name? It sounds made-up to me—like a character in a movie."

Brick shifted from one foot to the other, laughed nervously and said, "What do you mean? Why wouldn't I tell you my real name?"

"I don't know why. You tell me, Brick. You look a lot like the former tight end for the Seminole's football team. Didn't you just graduate from Florida State?"

Brick stammered a little and said, "Oh, uh I see the mistake. That was my, er, uh, my cousin. We get that a lot because we look alike."

"You are not a very good liar," Frances said with a smile. "I don't buy it. Why don't you tell me why you have been following us around and why you are using a phony name?"

Brick was disappointed. Five minutes with Frances Friday and he was discovered. He was a rookie at his job, and he was embarrassed at not being able to successfully complete his mission. He decided to explain everything and ask for her help. After a ten-minute discussion Frances left Brick and walked to the back of the store. She found Lady and Alexandra browsing among kitchen items.

Lady held up a large handmade pottery bowl. "Frances, what do you think? I think Ella and Auden would love this. You know how Ella likes unusual, artsy things with no practical purpose." Lady snickered and said under her breath, "Like her fiancé."

"I think Alexandra is clueless. That is what I think," said Frances.

"What?" said Alexandra, a little stunned by her aunt's abrupt statement.

Frances said in a hushed voice, "That boy did not follow us to the restaurant, walk into this shop, and start a conversation about hostess gifts because he wanted to talk to me."

"What do you mean?" asked Alexandra.

"He wants to talk to you," said Lady, laughing. "He probably had his dog trip you on purpose."

Alexandra looked over her aunt's shoulder at Brick, who was obviously stalling by fiddling with a display

73

of gourmet coffee beans. She told herself that such an attractive guy could not be interested in her. Just then Brick knocked over the display and coffee beans cascaded to the floor. He looked like he was dancing a soft shoe routine as he tried to quickly kick the beans under the cabinet away from his dog before she could eat them. This awkward display of clumsiness made her reconsider. She decided to overcome her diffidence and talk to him. "He is really cute. What do I say?"

"Here, take this bottle of balsamic glaze and tell him that this would be a very nice gift to bring to his friend's dinner party," said Frances. "And then start a conversation. He is obviously waiting to talk to you."

Alexandra's confidence was growing by the minute. She said, "What do I have to lose? I will probably never see him again anyway."

Frances said, "That's the spirit Alexandra! Take chances! Live your life! Except, well, actually you will see him again. Sooner than you think. I want you to go over there and ask him to be your date for the wedding."

"Frances!" Lady interjected. "I can't believe you are throwing Alexandra at strange men and inviting them to Ella's wedding. He could be a psycho-weirdo."

"He is not a psycho-weirdo. He is sort of a friend of a friend. I guarantee that if you ask him to be your plus-one at the wedding, he will accept," said Frances.

"I don't even know his name and you want me to ask him to be my date at the wedding?" said Alexandra.

"That is exactly what I want you to do. Trust me. Be brave and daring in your youth. His name is Brick Davis.

Here, take this and go!" Frances said as she pushed her niece toward the front of the store.

Alexandra reluctantly and shyly completed the mission. She had a brief conversation with Brick while her aunts continued browsing for gifts and nonchalantly observing. She was amazed at how willingly he accepted the invitation to attend the wedding with her on Saturday. She had a hunch that this guy had a hidden agenda, but she trusted her Aunt Frances. After all, it was just one date and Brick was a hunk. How bad could it be?

The three women walked back to the car with shopping bags in their hands and smiles on their faces. As they drove back to the hotel, Alexandra tried to ply her Aunt Frances with multiple questions about Brick Davis but was unsuccessful. Frances told her that Brick was a good guy and that she would have a good time, but she was purposely being vague. Her aunt would only reply, "I have my reasons. Just trust me." Alexandra finally gave up on questioning her aunt. She decided to have faith and go with it. She put her head back on the car headrest and enjoyed the ride back to The Breakers.

– Seven –
Thomas's Day Out

WHILE FRANCES, LADY, AND ALEXANDRA were on an adventure to hire a competent but unusual deejay, Thomas Friday lingered in his hotel room. He hoped that the wedding preparations were going well, but more importantly he hoped no one would ask him to do anything. Although his sisters were younger, they seemed to have taken positions of higher rank in the family. They often bossed him around and gave him things to do to occupy his time. As a result, he became very adept at sister avoidance. He entered the lobby café and asked the hostess to seat him at a table behind an impressive flower arrangement to hide him from view.

Finishing his breakfast and scanning the lobby in all directions for any sign of sisters, he darted quickly to the valet stand to retrieve his car. Thomas stood for a moment, fumbling through every pocket to find his valet ticket. The ticket was still by the phone on the desk in his room. The young attendant, noticing the obvious signs of a person who has misplaced their valet ticket and wanting to help, finally said, "Are you staying at the hotel, sir?"

"No, I am going out. I don't want to stay at the hotel. If I were staying here, I would be inside not here in the driveway waiting for my car," said Thomas. He gave a crumpled up dry cleaning ticket to the valet and thought to himself, "What a silly question. Who would stay inside on such a beautiful day?"

The attendant remembered this funny, disheveled man from the previous evening and so he sprinted off toward the parking lot. He quickly returned driving a sleek black Mercedes around the circle and up to the hotel entrance. He held the car door for Thomas, lingering a few moments for the customary tip. Thomas, a savvy traveler, picked up on the nonverbal cue and said, "Oh, here you are, young man," and handed him his empty coffee cup. He added, "Have you been to the Morikami Museum and Gardens?"

"No sir, I have never heard of it. I can probably get directions for you. Do you need directions?"

"Never heard of it?" said Thomas with surprise. He immediately lowered his opinion of this young man. A world-class example of a Japanese garden right in his hometown and he had never been, much less heard of it. What had become of the young people these days? He refused help with directions and set off on his adventure.

He drove south toward the gardens, enjoying the sunny day, the smooth ride of his car on the highway, and the peaceful feeling of being by himself. He really wanted to drive all the way to Fairchild Gardens in Coral Gables. It was a favorite spot when his business brought him to South Florida. He especially loved the butterfly garden and the orchid garden. Plus, Fairchild was the home of the American Orchid Society and he always felt at home among orchid folks. But this weekend, he chose the closer option so that he would be back in time for lunch. He was looking forward to exploring the many paths, rock gardens, bamboo groves, bonsai trees, and koi ponds at the Morikami. This was his first Japanese garden tour and he felt giddy, like a child on their first trip to Disney World.

Thomas was not the only person who had come to this garden for relaxation and refreshment. Maria Lopez, who worked at a nearby retirement home, also came to the gardens to find the peace and comfort that being close to nature provided. She was normally a joyful person, but a bad day at work the previous day had put her in a melancholy mood. Today was her day off so she awoke early, went for a run, got ready, and walked to her sister's house to pick up her nephew. She was excited to enjoy the gardens with him and let the landscape lighten her cares.

Thomas casually strolled along the path circling the lake, stopping now and then to listen to the audio tour through his earphones. He stopped and gazed at the rock garden. The large area of gravel was carefully raked in symmetrical lines and circles suggesting the movement of water. He was contemplating this unique style of gardening when Maria and her nephew quietly turned the corner around the high hedge and stood next to him.

Thomas, engrossed in the audio tour and thinking he was alone, was startled when he realized a woman was standing close to him. When he saw that she was an attractive woman, his heart started to race and he lost motor control. He tried to shuffle to the side to make room for them, but his two left feet tangled together and he tripped. He fell forward, disobeying the sign that clearly stated, "Please stay on the path." He stumbled into the intricate patterns of gravel, shuffling his feet and messing up several rows. He broke his fall and regained his balance by placing his hands on the large boulder in the middle of the garden. He stepped back onto the sidewalk and picked some gravel out of his shoe. At that moment, he could have sworn he heard the wind pick up and the bamboo start clanking together in disapproval of his disturbance in the garden's balance.

Mumbling and fumbling with his words he said, "I am so sorry. I tripped on the ... Who should I call? Should I call someone?" Looking around for help, he added, "Do you see a rake anywhere?"

Maria said, "Qué?" in her native Spanish tongue.

"Oh, you speak Spanish. Let's see if I can remember my Spanish." Thomas spoke in a slow, loud voice, "I am muy embarass ... embaraz ... muy embarazado. Yes I think that is it." He was trying to convey that he was embarrassed and that he was not the type of person that went into peaceful garden settings and wreaked havoc on the landscape. Thomas was feeling nervous and started to sweat profusely. He looked up at the sun and said, "Is it me or is it getting hot today? Uh, er, uh, estoy caliente."

The woman giggled, and he noticed how pretty she looked smiling. He did not know that she was laughing at the fact that he had just told her he was pregnant. To make matters worse, he made the common mistake of claiming to be an attractive man instead of communicating that his body temperature was rising in the warm sun.

Thomas bashfully put his hands in his pockets and tried to think of something else to say. As he looked down, he noticed his pants looked old and wrinkled. He wished he had dressed better today. He noticed a rip in his pocket and instead of saying something intelligent, he said, "I tore the fábrica on my pantallones," which in Spanish actually meant, "I tore the factory on my pants."

Maria did not feel it was necessary to tell this man his language errors. Neither did she feel it was necessary to tell him that she was fluent in English. She was feeling her melancholy mood lifting. What else might this funny man say? She would have an amusing story to tell at the dinner table. All she had to do was to keep the conversation going and keep Thomas speaking Spanish.

Thomas interpreted her friendly smile and laughter as encouragement. He told himself that he had obviously gotten off to a good start by speaking her native language, so he continued the conversation. "This is a fine example of a late period jardin de roca—rock garden," he said emphatically pointing to the gravel as if to use the universal sign language of the pointing finger to make all things clear.

"Sí, rock garden," Maria agreed.

Feeling the conversation was at a standstill and wanting to continue to get to know this woman, Thomas's brain suddenly produced some Spanish phrases from deep within his memory. He said, "What is your name? Er, uh, cómo te llamas?"

"Me llamo Maria," said Maria.

"Maria, what a lovely name. It is nice to meet you, Maria. My name is … er uh, mi llamo … or is it nombre es Tomás."

"Mucho gusto en conocerte, Tomás," said Maria, meaning nice to meet you Thomas. She pointed to the young boy. "Éste es mi sobrino, Carlos," meaning this is my nephew Carlos.

Thomas was lost on what gusto, conocerte or sobrino meant but said politely, "Sí, muy bien. Maria and Carlos." He added another, "muy bien," for good measure. Wanting to get to know if she was fond of gardening he asked, "Er ,uh do you like los jardineros?"

"Sí, me gustan los jardines," said Maria smiling.

"Muy bien, muy bien," said Thomas. Feeling the strain on his brain, he felt perplexed and frustrated at the language barrier keeping him from getting to know this charming gardener. He ran through the Spanish phrases he learned in high school but none of them seemed right for the circumstance. He could hardly get to know her with mi professor es inteligente (my teacher is smart) or mi libro de la biblioteca es rojo (my library book is red). Or more useless were the few phrases he learned during his travels like dónde esta tu auto (where is your car) or aceptan tarjetas de crédito (do you take credit cards). She may totally misinterpret those sentences and slap his face and walk away, or worse, call security.

Maria broke the tension by telling Thomas she was

thirsty and asked if he wanted to get a drink. "Tengo sed, quieres tomar un refresco?" she said making the drinking motion with her hand to her mouth.

He was disappointed at her hand motions implying someone drinking. He desperately wanted her to know he was not drunk. Thomas suddenly remembered a phrase from his college spring break days in Mexico and said it with a little indignation in his voice, "No! Um … no estoy borracho. I have not been drinking."

Maria could not fake it anymore. She burst out laughing and said, "Thomas, you are so funny. I wanted to know if you would like to get a drink at the café. I am getting a little hot in the sun. You know, tengo calor, not estoy caliente and I am thirsty, tengo sed," she said, gently correcting his Spanish.

Thomas blurted out, "You speak English!" He was not sure if he was more relieved that he could communicate or upset that she had let him struggle with Spanish. "Yes, by all means, let's go to the café and get a drink," he said, delighted that they would spend more time together. Thomas, against Maria's protest, bought her and Carlos a drink and a few snacks. They sat at a table overlooking the lake and enjoyed small plates of salted edamame and egg rolls and sipped on iced tea and lemonade.

"Where are you from, Maria?" asked Thomas.

"I am from Puerto Rico. I came here years ago to go to nursing school but kind of got sidetracked."

"What do you mean sidetracked, if you don't mind my asking?"

"I don't mind. I have a big family; most of them are

still in Puerto Rico. I moved here with my sister and started college. My grandparents became ill and my family sent them to live with us. My parents lost their business and are still trying to rebuild so they can't help care for them. I took a job at a senior home to get the employee discount to help pay for their care. So, my education got put on hold." She said with a little sadness in her voice, "And, I never went back and finished."

"Are you also taking care of Carlos?" asked Thomas.

"Only one or two days a week. My sister is a single mother and works long hours and needs my help. I enjoy spending time with Carlos. He is a great kid." She looked at Carlos, who was getting a little bored and was trying to balance his straw on his upper lip.

Thomas did not know what to say. He was impressed that this woman had given up her dreams to help her family. He had never experienced the hardship of giving up his own ambitions to help other people. His first wife's illness and death was definitely a trial, but he had more than enough family members with the time and energy to help him through it.

Changing the subject away from her problems, which is the reason she came to the garden in the first place, she asked Thomas, "Do you live in the area?"

"No, I'm here to attend my niece's wedding. It's in Palm Beach on Saturday. I'm from the other coast of Florida—Sarasota area. I like to visit gardens in different areas of the state when I can. I've really enjoyed this garden, although I would have liked to go to Fairchild but I didn't have the time today."

"Fairchild is beautiful and I especially love the orchid garden. You live near the Marie Selby Gardens, don't you? They have an extensive collection of epiphytes if I am not mistaken. I would like to see it someday."

Thomas was astounded. Which one of the last three statements out of this woman's mouth was more astounding he could not decide. She had been to Fairchild Gardens. She had heard of Marie Selby's epiphyte collection. She even seemed to know what an epiphyte was. He was speechless and it showed, as his jaw became slack and hung down a few inches.

Maria felt comfortable and at ease with this fellow gardener. She continued, "I am a bit of a novice at growing orchids. I like to try different varieties of orchids at home to see which will grow best indoors. If I am successful I put them in little pots and place them in the residents' rooms, especially those who don't have any decorations or green things in their space. I think it cheers people up to see a beautiful flower, don't you? In fact, my workplace is next to a garden center and when I am having a stressful day, I take a break and walk to the garden center to relax among the plants."

Thomas was again speechless. He had always enjoyed gardening for the sole purpose of pleasing himself. He had never thought of his hobby as a way of helping or bringing joy to other people. Hearing Maria's story, he became a little ashamed thinking of how he would not let neighborhood children into his immaculately landscaped yard. He had even put up a sign that said "keep out" at the entrance to his garden during Halloween so that trick-or-treaters would stay away. What kind of selfish, plant hoarding monster had he become?

He realized that his silence was causing an awkward pause in the conversation and, wanting it to continue, he finally said, "You are right. I think flowers and plants bring people great happiness. I know they do for me. You should come to Sarasota and visit Selby Gardens sometime." Thomas was not usually bold, but he added, "I would be happy to go with you." Then probing further, trying to be subtle, he added, "Does your boyfriend like gardens? He is welcome to join us as well."

"Oh, I don't have a boyfriend, not right now anyway. I would love to see Sarasota sometime," said Maria in a wistful voice, emphasizing the word "sometime," meaning that she could not see such a trip happening anytime in the near future.

Thomas was thrilled at the news that Maria did not have a boyfriend. But he was not sure how to bridge the gap between just meeting this woman and inviting her to be his guest in Sarasota. He changed the subject to keep the conversation going. "My family develops and manages senior care facilities all over Florida. I think I'll tell them that they should put orchids in every resident's room. It's a wonderful idea."

Maria was pleased that Thomas appreciated her idea, and she did not think he was being insincere about using it in his family business. She did not have time to say so because Carlos, who had been quiet up to this point, was now screaming for help. He had defied the laws of physics and somehow wedged his head in between the metal railings that surrounded the café and gotten stuck.

Maria jumped up and calmed him down, tilted his head at the right angle and slipped it out intact. He began the prelude to a powerful cry. Young children often have a way of derailing the conversation and bringing it to an abrupt end. A wise mother or caregiver heeds this notification that the meeting has come to an end. Maria scooped up Carlos and headed for the exit before his cry could reach full measure. She called back to Thomas over her shoulder, "Thank you for the drink and snacks. I should get Carlos home. It was nice meeting you, Thomas."

Thomas replied, "Nice to meet you too. Adios, Maria." Thomas stood alone in the café with his hand still waving in the air. He was saddened that their friendship was going to end as suddenly as it began.

– Eight –
Freddie Friday Arrives

THE FRIDAY FAMILY GATHERED in the hotel bar for an afternoon drink. They were toasting the good fortune of finding a new deejay and praising Frances, Lady, and Alexandra's quick work. As Thomas pulled up a chair and ordered his drink, Frances asked him, "Where did you go today?"

Thomas answered, "I went to the Morikami Museum and Gardens."

"That sounds interesting. What did you like about it?" asked Frances.

"It is a fine example of a Japanese garden not far from here. It was founded by a group of Japanese farmers in the early twentieth century. The Yamato Colony, as it was called, was abandoned but the gardens and the museum are still there. And, I met the most interesting woman there! She knows all about epiphytes. You don't meet a woman like that every day."

"Well thank God we don't," jibed Deidre's husband Max, who was quick with the one-liners and also fond of ribbing Thomas.

Thomas ignored his brother-in-law. He was usually good humored about Max's teasing, but on the subject of gardening and gardeners he did not like flippancy. "She was remarkable ... and from Puerto Rico too," he added. He raised his voice and addressed all the family members assembled at the table. "By the way, what does embarazado mean in Spanish?"

Deidre, who excelled at languages, was the first to answer. "It means to be pregnant. What silly questions you ask. Why on earth do you need to know that Spanish word?"

"Is someone suing you for patrimony?" said Max, half joking and half serious.

Thomas reviewed his attempted conversation in Spanish with Maria as he drove back to the hotel. He had the sinking feeling that he had inadvertently told Maria that he was pregnant. Now it was confirmed. This certainly explained why she had laughed at him. If he was a stronger man, and belonged to a different family, he would share the humorous translation error and they all would have a good laugh and it would be forgotten. His experience growing up with the Friday siblings told him that, in his case, it would most certainly not be forgotten. At future family gatherings, especially after alcohol was applied, someone would undoubtedly tease him saying, "Hey, Thomas, how is the pregnancy coming?" Or "Hey, Thomas, is it a boy or a girl?" Or worse, "Hey, Thomas, do you know who the mother is?" He was not a person that could easily laugh at himself, so he kept his language misstep to himself.

Deidre scowled and said in a worried voice, "Was the woman you met today pregnant? Why would she be talking to you about being pregnant? You are not bringing a strange pregnant woman that you just met at a garden to the wedding, are you?"

"She is not strange!" said Thomas emphatically. "And she is not pregnant! Well, as far as I know. Of course I'm not completely sure. You can never really be sure of something like that. I find it is better not to ask about those things when you don't know someone very well. One time I saw my neighbor at a party and asked her when her baby was due. She put her hands on her hips told me in the most irritated voice that she had her baby two months earlier. Then she walked off in a huff and hasn't spoken to me since. And when she is out walking her dog and I drive by, she doesn't even wave back but gives me a dirty look. I think neighbors should wave to each other no matter what their differences, don't you? It's so unsettling when a neighbor does not wave to you. I feel …"

Deidre cut short her brother's ramblings and said impatiently, "Thomas! If you are bringing a guest to the wedding at this late hour, I need to know."

Lady chimed in, "It's bad manners to add guests to the wedding list at the last minute. The numbers have already been given to the caterer."

Frances said, "I'm sure the caterer typically plans for a few more. It will probably be alright."

Thomas said, "Well, I haven't asked her yet but I will. I have to think of the best way to do it. You know meeting new people is hard for me and I don't like to be hasty. Remember that woman I met in Las Vegas. How was I to know she was really ..."

Frances interrupted him before he wandered into another long story. She wanted to prevent his sisters from bludgeoning him, so she asked, "Why don't you call her right now and ask her to the wedding?"

"Well I don't have her phone number. What was I supposed to do say 'Hello my name is Thomas what is your phone number?' I just met her; what would she think? These things take time." Thomas looked at Deidre. "Go ahead and put down a plus-one for me. How do you say wedding in Spanish?"

Thomas felt his sisters' eyes on him. Over the years, they had perfected the art of glaring at him with disapproval. He felt very uncomfortable and ran his finger around his collar. Luckily a distraction presented itself that shifted the attention away from him. The distraction was the arrival of the Friday family's youngest brother, Frederick, or Freddie, as his family called him.

Freddie would fit the description of most tall, dark, and handsome men that appear in popular romance novels. He had skin that tanned easily, a fit body that wore resort wear perfectly, straight whitened teeth, and a dark head of hair that was thinning ever so slightly. He was the salesman for the Friday family business, so his people skills and likeability factor were very high. He was wearing a flowery silk shirt, shorts, and sandals, which were elegantly accessorized with an expensive watch.

"Are we speaking Spanish," said Freddie introducing

himself into the group. "Well then, hola mi familia. Donde esta the lovely bride, my beautiful niece Ella?"

"Hello, Freddie," said Deidre. "Ella is picking up some of her bridesmaids at the airport."

Frances remarked, "Freddie, you look fabulous, have you been to the health resort again?"

"No, just doing a little less of this," said Freddie making an eating motion, "and more of this," swinging his arms like a running motion. "I have also been playing a lot of golf and tennis, so my tan is at its finest. I did not want to spoil the wedding pictures for my baby sister's big event," said Freddie, giving his sister Deidre a brotherly smooch on top of her head.

Lady looked past her brother, searching for someone. "Freddie, I can't believe you do not have a date to the wedding. It is so unlike you not to have a girl on your arm."

"Well, sister dear, I am still licking my wounds from getting tossed by my third wife. I am a free man, so I am going solo this weekend."

"I'm so sorry to hear about your divorce," said Frances.

"Thank you, Frances," said Freddie. He moved around the table to stand behind her chair and gave her shoulders an appreciative squeeze. "I guess to get sympathy in this family, I will have to look to the in-laws."

Freddie noticed Alexandra sitting among his relatives. "Who is this lovely lady? Is this little Alexandra that has been freed from the lonely tower in the northeast and now reunited with her family in the land of sunshine?"

"Hello, Uncle Freddie," said Alexandra. She slowly stood up and held out her hand for a handshake.

"Do you even remember me, child?" said Freddie. He ignored her outstretched hand and stepped forward and gave her a big bear hug.

"I have some memories of you at the beach, but they are fuzzy," Alexandra admitted.

"Well of course, you were only eight when the Friday family ban was put in place. We will be best pals by the end of the weekend," said Freddie taking a seat in between Alexandra and Deidre.

The conversation continued among the family members. Deidre covered the itinerary with Freddie and the other family members. They filled him in on the recent deejay crisis and how Frances came to the rescue with Dylan. Freddie looked at Deidre and said, "I will not be around tonight for wedding festivities. Count me out."

"Why not?" protested Deidre.

"Sorry, Sis. It can't be avoided. I'm going to Lance's birthday party."

"Which one of your ex, uh, ex-children is Lance?" asked Thomas. "Is he your first wife's second son?"

Lady interrupted, "No. Lance is Freddie's second wife's third son."

"No, no, no," corrected Freddie. "Lance is my third wife's first son. You know my wife Susan?"

Thomas looked perplexed. "I get your exes all so confused. Is Susan the one that had the little pig named Tiffany?"

This time Frances corrected him. "No, Tiffany was the name of Freddie's second wife. The first wife had the pig. Susan has all the little dogs."

"That's right," said Freddie. "My third wife, Susan, would never own or go near a pig. Susan is the one with the gaggle of prize-winning Pekingese dogs."

Correct categorization of flora and fauna was important to Thomas. "Are a group of Pekingese dogs called a gaggle?"

"No, a gaggle refers to a group of geese," said Frances.

"Does Susan have geese as well? I didn't know people kept those as pets. My goodness, she does love animals. Are her geese just here for the winter or are they here year-round?" asked Thomas.

Lady spoke over Thomas, ignoring him. "I also get your ex-wives, ex-children, and ex-pets confused. You need to make us a chart."

Max was entertained by this conversation and could not resist another joke. "Everyone knows Freddie's philosophy in life is to eat, drink, and remarry."

Freddie had married and was subsequently divorced by three women who already had children from previous relationships. As a result, he had three ex-wives, five ex-stepchildren, six ex-step dogs, and an ex-step pig as of this book's publication. He would say that all his divorces were amicable and that he still had fond feelings toward all his exes. He was a kind stepdad and genuinely liked his exes' children, owing to the fact that he did not help very much in the child rearing. His role was more like a doting grandfather or uncle than a real dad. Freddie and the stepchildren had a special camaraderie and he had a particular sympathy for them, knowing their mothers as he did. He remembered their birthdays and sent cards or presents on special occasions.

Ignoring snide remarks, Freddie looked at Alexandra. "Susan is my third wife who just gave me the push six months ago. She is throwing her son Lance a twenty-first birthday party at a chic restaurant to celebrate his entrance into manhood and his legal right to get sloshed. I promised I would be there. He seemed very anxious that I come. I don't mind telling you that it made me feel good that it was so important to him for me to be there. Don't want to disappoint the young man on this milestone birthday."

"Anxious for you to come?" said Lady. "He must want to borrow money." Lady was in the habit of reading between the lines and determining motives. Her family had to admit that she had a knack for calling situations the right way. She had observed Lance as a young boy. He would work the family gatherings by asking everyone for a quarter. She was sure that by the time Susan divorced Freddie, Lance had amassed a small fortune off the Friday relatives, one quarter at a time.

Freddie turned toward Lady and rolled his eyes. "Oh Lady, you are such a cynic. I think I made a good impression on the boy and he is facing manhood as a twenty-one-year-old without a father figure or male role model. I'm hurt by your sarcasm."

Frances jumped into the conversation like a mother separating arguing siblings. This was a habit she developed since joining the Friday family. She tried to change the subject but unintentionally touched on another sore spot. "Who got the Boca Raton beach house in the divorce? I hope you did. You put so much work into that house. It was so beautiful."

"No! Susan got the Boca beach house, although technically it is still in my name for a few more weeks. And she changed the locks and won't let me get my things. I left three expensive watches there and she will not give them back. I told her I thought that was unfair. My other wives gave those watches to me as gifts, so they belong to me. After all a gift is a gift. Susan did not agree and said she was keeping my things as some sort of bad husband tax."

Lady was tired of hearing Freddie drone on about his exes. "Enough about your failed marriages! We are here to celebrate Ella's marriage and we don't need you to sour the mood with your sad stories. Don't go on about your divorces in front of Auden's family. They will think we are dysfunctional and can't keep commitments."

"You are absolutely right, Ladybug," said Freddie, calling his sister by the nickname she loathed. "I can't help myself when I get going on my ex-helpmates' shortcomings. It is hard to stop but I will remember that when Ella is around." Changing his tone, he declared, "Marriage is a wonderful institution." Freddie glanced quickly across the table at his brother-in-law Max.

Without missing a beat Max said, "But who wants to live in an institution?"

Freddie, Max, and Alexandra laughed as the rest of

the family rolled their eyes. Freddie looked at his watch and finished his drink. "I have to run. Tootles everyone."

Freddie jumped into his convertible Audi and headed for a very pricey restaurant in a very hip neighborhood in Fort Lauderdale. He chose valet parking because that was the only option. Everyone who is anyone knows that the trendy restaurants are in inconvenient locations and always lack adequate parking. If patrons want roadside visibility, easy access, ample, free parking, and a legible menu, they should go to Cracker Barrel. It did not bother Freddie because he knew that it is worth the aggravation to see and be seen at the chic restaurant.

He pushed open the rustic doors of the restaurant and walked through the crowded dining space into the private room reserved for Lance's party. The party was just getting started and the room was buzzing with beautiful, socially conscious young people helping themselves to gluten-free, sugar-free, vegan organic small plates, all courtesy of Freddie's ex-wife Susan. Freddie tried not to think about the recent divorce settlement and that his former dollars were being spent on this elegant soiree. He had a habit of putting negative thoughts out of his mind and concentrating on the positive. He told himself to forgive and forget and enjoy the party.

He attempted to start a conversation with a girl who was absorbed in her cell phone. He opened the lines of communication with small talk. "I hear they have a killer faux salmon appetizer here."

The girl lifted her head from her phone and looked at him with a look approaching disgust. "No one says 'killer' anymore," she said. "That word is offensive."

"Sorry. I meant to say that I heard the fake salmon appetizer was very good."

But the girl had walked away before he finished clarifying his point. Freddie, having been born with a confident nature, natural affability, and the personality of an extrovert, was not discouraged by his first failed conversation of the night.

He moved to a young man who was standing alone. He opened the conversation with a simple introduction this time, "Hello, I am Freddie Friday, Lance's ex-stepdad."

Freddie was relieved that this man did not bite his head off and scurry away. Instead, he stepped into Freddie's personal space and started shaking his head up and down and looking intently into Freddie's face. He remained there for an uncomfortably long period of time. The man finally said, "Yeah, now I can see the family resemblance. At first I did not see it, but now I can tell you are definitely Lance's stepdad." And then he walked away without introducing himself or continuing the conversation.

Freddie preferred short conversations when trying to work a room, but this was getting ridiculous. Looking around he spotted a heated discussion among three people. He walked over and inserted himself into the conversation, listening and nodding. They were arguing about the rising cost of guitars and how the government should tax non-musicians to pay for musical instruments for aspiring songwriters. Freddie listened sympathetically for a while and, having no opinion on the subject, he left the circle and walked up to the bar to order a drink.

His ex-wife Susan walked up to the bar to speak with the bartender. Even though their relationship was naturally strained, he was actually glad to see a familiar, if not friendly face. He turned toward her with a smile and said, "Thanks for the invite, Susie. I'm glad there are no hard feelings and we can let bygones be bygones. We are all mature adults, right?"

Susan spoke to Freddie in an all too familiar harping tone. "You know I hate being called Susie and there are plenty of hard feelings still. Lance wanted to invite you against my advice. And as for you being a mature adult, that is debatable."

"Oh, those are harsh words ex-love of my life," said Freddie in a fake dejected voice. "I'm here now, so let's make the best of it. Let's bury the hatchet. Let's agree to disagree. Let's mend fences and trade olive branches and all that." Freddie stopped talking because he had run out of synonymous phrases for making peace. He also stopped because he noticed a murderous look come into Susan's eyes.

Realizing her temper was flaring and remembering what her therapist said about stress triggers, Susan forced a smile and said, "I'm glad that you could make it to the party."

"I'm happy to be here for Lance. How is he doing these days?"

"He is still living at home and does not have a job, but other than that he is terrific." Susan's voice had a sarcastic tone, but Freddie detected the sound of a mother who feels helpless.

Freddie softened to her. "Lots of people live with their parents nowadays until they get established. Does he pay you rent? My parents made me pay market rent and do odd jobs around the house so I wouldn't live with them forever. Don't worry about Lance; he will be fine."

Susan softened her tone as well. "I hope you're right. I don't make him pay rent but I've given him the responsibility of taking care of my dogs, especially since I am traveling so much lately. I'm hoping he learns responsibility doing that." Looking toward the door she said, "Enjoy the party, Freddie. I have to welcome the guests."

Freddie scanned the room. He noticed he was the only person besides Susan who was over twenty-five. This added to his fatherly feelings toward Lance. He thought to himself, "Lady could not have been more wrong. Borrow money from me indeed." This young man had obviously reached out to him in a desperate cry for fatherly affirmation on this important day. He was very glad he had come to support his ex-stepson.

Lance spotted Freddie across the room and made a beeline for him. He greeted Freddie with a fist bump.

"Hi, old man, glad you could come," said Lance. Freddie had never achieved the status of being called "dad" in his relationship with Lance.

Freddie said with ex-step fatherly affection, "Wouldn't miss it, Lance." Looking around the room he added, "Looks like everyone is having a good time."

Lance put his hand on Freddie's shoulder and quickly got down to business. "Hey, old man. My friends and I are holding a bicycle rally protest in a few days and could really use your help."

"Really, how exciting. What social injustice are you riding for?"

Lance explained, "We call ourselves VAKCT. It stands for vegans against killing Christmas trees. We are riding our bikes around town in Christmas sweaters trying to call attention to ourselves because we want people to switch to artificial trees."

Freddie was not up on social causes and was a little confused. He asked, "What does 'vegan' have to do with Christmas trees?"

"Nothing really. But no one signed up for the protest so we added the word 'vegan' in the title. Now we have over a hundred people coming."

Freddie was touched. He could see himself riding his expensive road bike alongside these young activists, and it warmed his heart to be included. "I will be there by your side! I will even hold a sign, paint my body, dress up or whatever protesters are doing these days."

"That's awesome! I knew I could count on you. But, uh, I don't actually need you to come to the protest. I was thinking that you could loan us some money to help fund the cause. Can I borrow twenty-five thousand dollars?"

There it was. The big ask. The reason he had been

invited to the party. All became clear. The scales fell from Freddie's eyes. He was still staggering thinking of the amount of the request. "That is a lot of flyers and poster board. I did not realize protesting rang up such hefty expenses."

"Well, I could use the money for other causes. I'm involved in a ton of good causes," said Lance piously. "My mother claims she is short on cash since the divorce."

Freddie thought to himself, "Short on cash, my eye." He knew exactly how much cash his ex-wife had extracted from him in the divorce. He also knew that when Lance said "other causes" that was code for keeping Lance from having to hold down a steady job. Freddie felt uneasy. What does a man do in this situation? Parenting books don't have a chapter labeled "What to do when your unemployed ex-stepson asks for huge sums of money to support his ever-changing causes." Most of all Freddie was embarrassed that he had been invited to the party solely for his money. He was also a little irritated that Lady was right.

Several of Lance's friends gathered around to hear Freddie's answer. His name came up frequently at fund-raising discussions at the coffee shop. What they did not know was that Freddie Friday was a master of deflection and doublespeak. Being a successful salesman and having three very querulous and demanding wives had taught him the best way to answer a question without com-mitting to anything. Freddie said generously and with a forced smile on his face, "Of course. I will see what I can do. I can't think of any reason not to help you in this worthy cause."

"Awesome. I'll be in touch," Lance said as he gave Freddie a high five. Lance and all his friends seemed pleased. They walked away and did not speak to Freddie the rest of the evening. Feeling that he had served his purpose, he left the party before the quinoa and black bean birthday cake was served.

Driving back to The Breakers, he thought of many reasons not to help Lance's worthy cause. For one, he did not have liquid assets amounting to twenty-five thousand dollars. For another, he knew that his ex-stepson would keep coming back to him for loans if he funded him this time.

He pulled off the interstate an exit early and stopped by Howleys to grab a bite to eat. Even though he helped himself to a generous number of appetizers at the party, he was not satisfied. He was upset, and a full stomach was the cure. As he enjoyed his burger he started to feel better. He thought, "That is probably why Lance's friends at the party were so unfriendly. They were just plain hungry."

– Nine –
Bachelorette Party

ELLA'S WISH CAME TRUE and the bachelorette party came together at the last minute. All the bridesmaids in the group chat were told to meet near the pool by the beach bungalows just before sunset. Frances and Lady arrived early to the party because they always arrived early to events and because they knew that Deidre and Ella always arrived late to events. As Frances stood in the beautiful beachfront setting, she watched the hotel staff scurrying around preparing for the party. She was also relieved that Dylan had arrived and was already playing party music. She thought to herself, "this turned out well."

Frances noticed Alexandra coming towards them. To Frances, her niece looked very different from the girl she had met in the courtyard the day before. She put her arm around her niece and said, "You are looking especially cheerful this evening and you look adorable in that sundress."

Alexandra considered this statement. "You are right. I am cheerful. I don't know why but since I have been here, I feel happier. I guess it is the beautiful weather. If

I were back up north, I would be freezing and wearing a sweatshirt all day. Now I am going to a party at the beach in a sundress."

Not long after all the bridesmaids, family members, and friends arrived, the bride and her mother made their dilatory entrance to the party. Frances intercepted Deidre and Ella and introduced them to their new wedding deejay.

"We are so happy that you were available at the last minute," Deidre said to Dylan. "You are a lifesaver. Ella is so excited about this party."

Dylan smiled and looked at Ella. "Tonight's the night! You look like the happiest girl in the whole USA." Addressing the other women in the crowd he added, "Isn't she lovely?"

Ella blushed and was pleased. She asked Dylan what type of songs he was going to play for the party. She wanted to make sure the music was not lame. He answered with confidence. "I'm not going to play any silly love songs. I'm going to play that funky music. We are going to get down tonight. So put on your dancin' shoes."

Ella did not understand anything that Dylan said but she had a good feeling about him. She could tell within minutes of meeting someone if they were legit and she thought to herself this guy is totally legit. She felt a good connection with her deejay and that was all that mattered to her.

Deidre sighed, looking up at the palm trees waving

in the breeze. "It's such a nice evening for a bachelorette party. The clouds have cleared and the sun is shining."

Dylan agreed. "It's another day in paradise. I can see clearly now; in fact I can see for miles and miles."

As the women walked away from the deejay table, Deidre told Frances, "I like Dylan. He is the perfect deejay for our wedding. There is something so familiar and melodious about the way he speaks. You have such interesting friends, Frances."

While Frances, Lady, and Deidre stood by the beach bungalows chatting and watching the younger generation enjoy themselves, two young women dressed in strange costumes walked into the party. They were wearing black leggings, black and white striped tee shirts, black suspenders, red berets, and black ballet slippers. They had theatrical white makeup on their faces with little black diamonds around their eyes and bright red lipstick on their lips.

Deidra was alarmed. "Who are they? What are they doing here?"

Frances explained, "Remember when Auden's mother asked if his cousins that live in Palm Beach could do a pantomime at the wedding reception?"

"Yes, we told them absolutely not. Can you imagine what people would think if clowns showed up at the wedding?" said Deidre.

Lady clarified. "Mimes are not really clowns. It is a different art form."

Frances continued, "I had to make a deal with Auden's mother last night. She agreed to fire Debbie the deejay if we said yes to the mimes. Evidently, the performing arts run strong in the Woods family. To improve relations with your future in-laws, I took it upon myself to offer this gesture of goodwill. However, I suggested to her that the Woods cousins should do their pantomime at the bachelorette party instead of the wedding reception. What could it hurt? I understand that mimes don't make much noise and people may not even notice them."

"Frances! Why would you agree to that?" Deidre screamed in a hushed voice. "His mother is asking too much. What will Ella's friends think?"

Frances justified her decision. "You should really be thanking me that I drew the line at pantomimes. The Woods family also has cousins that live in Okeechobee that are banjoists. I held firm and said no to the banjoists."

"I only hope they don't get made fun of," said Lady. "Some of Ella's school friends may be snooty. Do young people even know what pantomime is?"

"It will be fine," said Frances reassuringly. She did not exactly believe that it would be fine, but the promise was made, the mimes were at the party in costume and there was no point in concentrating on the negatives. Now was the time to welcome the mimes with open arms and hope for the best.

Deidre acquiesced. There was no way to get rid the mimes now. She pondered out loud. "Is it better to have the mimes perform before or after sunset or should they do their thing off to the side the whole time? I have no precedent. I've never been to a party with mimes. I'll go ask Dylan what he thinks. He is in show business. Maybe he will have a suggestion."

Frances interrupted. "I'll go talk to Dylan. Let me handle it, Deidre. You just enjoy the party." Frances did not want Deidre to spend time with Dylan. She might notice his odd way of speaking and start to worry about his abilities as a deejay. The last thing she wanted was to upset the mother of the bride.

Deidre said, "I will go talk to Dylan. I can manage the situation myself." She smiled at Frances with a confident smile. "You are not the only problem solver in this family." She walked toward the deejay table and got Dylan's attention. "Dylan, I suppose you saw the mimes walk by."

Dylan smiled and said, "The short people in the raspberry berets?"

"Yes, those are the mimes. They are relatives of the groom and Frances, against my wishes, agreed to let them perform at the bachelorette party. There is nothing I can do now but make the best of it. I'm not sure where to fit them into the program. What do you think?"

"It don't matter to me. I'll do anything for you," said Dylan.

"Let me see," said Deidre concentrating. "What is the best time for a pantomime?"

"Rainy days and Mondays are the only time I can think of," said Dylan.

"You are quite right. There is dramatic, melancholy side to mimes that may bring the party down. Maybe we should save their performance until the end. Oh, why did Frances ever agree to this?"

"I feel for you. It's a shame. If you could turn back time," commiserated Dylan.

Deidre threw her hands up in the air. "I'll leave it up to you facilitate their performance. Please make sure it flows well with the night's activities."

"I'm your man. You can count on me," said Dylan with confidence.

Deidre liked this young man. She liked a capable person of action who did not fall apart when strange requests, like an unexpected pantomime, were thrown at him at the last minute. She walked away quite content and gratified that she had solved the latest problem.

Brandy, one of Ella's bridesmaids, wandered away from the crowd and headed toward the deejay table. She leaned over the table towards Dylan, smiling and giggling for no apparent reason. Dylan was trying hard to ignore her and focus on his duties. She finally stepped in front of him and said, "I'm Brandy. Do you want to get together later tonight?"

Dylan had lost count of the hyper-aggressive young women that approached him at weddings. He communicated his lack of interest to her by saying, "Does your mother know?"

Brandy was insulted that Dylan was treating her like a child and said, "I am a grown woman. I just wanted to know if you would buy me a drink later."

He replied, "Brandy, you're a fine girl. Baby, don't get hooked on me. Get back to the party."

"You are such a jerk," Brandy said. She turned, with wounded vanity, and made a dramatic exit.

Dylan was used to this type of immature reaction. However, he did not want to be rude to party guests so he said, "Why can't we be friends?"

Ella asked Dylan to announce that at this point in the party they would head to the beach for pictures and to watch the sunset. There is a phenomenon that occurs on Florida beaches just before sunset. No matter which coast, as the sun sinks in the sky, the lighting becomes magical. The partygoers took advantage of this "golden hour" and snapped away with their phone cameras. There were shots, posted later on social media, of Ella with her bridesmaids; Ella with family members; Ella and friends jumping in the air. Even the cousin-mimes joined in the fun by pretending to walk along the beach but not really moving forward. All this physical activity on the beach combined with the magnificent colors in the sky put every partygoer in a great mood.

As the partygoers came back into the bungalow area, Dylan matched the joyful mood with the next round of songs. He announced that they would have lip-synch contest and asked who wanted to go first. Ten girls grabbed for the microphone and most were requesting bad boyfriend songs. Dylan was not surprised by their requests and thought of Shakespeare's line, "Hell hath no fury like a woman scorned." He would have added "and a woman scorned likes to sing about it." He handed the microphone to the clamoring girls and played the requested songs.

Alexandra was slowly coming out of her shell, but she was not ready to sing in front of Ella's friends. She looked for her family members in the crowd. As she approached the deejay table, she could not believe her eyes. Dylan and Frances were talking to Brick Davis.

She interrupted the conversation. "What are you doing here?"

"I work at The Breakers part time, in the beach bungalows," answered Brick nonchalantly. "Dylan was giving me some instructions." Before he rushed away to continue his duties Brick blurted out, "You look great, Alexandra!"

Looking at Frances, Alexandra said, "Brick seems to be everywhere we are. Isn't that interesting, Aunt Frances?"

Frances answered with a mischievous smile, "It is a small world, isn't it."

Alexandra tried to question her aunt again but did not get a sufficient explanation because Dylan started to make an announcement to the crowd. He asked the partygoers to turn their attention poolside for a special tribute to the bride. He started the music to "All You Need is Love" by the Beatles.

The cousin-mimes, a little rusty at first, started moving around in a kind of swaying motion and making hearts with their hands when the word "love" came up in the song. Dylan, being a performer, knew that the pantomime needed a little something extra. He had instructed Brick to watch for his signal. He gave it halfway through the song. Brick passed by the pantomime with a fresh tray of appetizers, did a clumsy, fake trip and pushed the mimes into the pool.

The crowd, which had not been paying much attention, turned to see what had caused the loud splash. At first everyone was startled and wanted to know how a mime would react. Would they break silence and finally say something? Would they curse or cry out for help? Would they put on their angry faces and act out frustration by shaking their fists at Brick? Everyone watched breathlessly to see the mimes' reaction.

Looking up from water, still a little startled, the mimes saw every party guest, hotel staff, and other onlookers staring down at them. It was their biggest audience to date. For the first time that evening, they had everyone's attention. They could not resist the urge to continue to perform. It is what a mime, and especially mimes fond of improvisational humor, live for.

Taking advantage of the stage they now found themselves on, or better yet in, they started to act out that they were drowning—flailing their arms and putting their hands to their mouths and mouthing silently the words "Help! Help!" in an exaggerated way. Then they started trying to climb on top of each other to get out of the pool in a funny fake panic mode. When they finally scrambled out of the pool they did a dramatic kicking motion toward Brick's behind as he was passing by again with a tray of drinks.

Their drama coach would have been proud. Remembering her words that you should end your performance leaving the audience wanting more, they ran off the pool deck, exiting stage right. The assembled audience cheered and clapped. They were impressed at the mimes' good-natured attempt to overlook the offense and their quick thinking of how to turn an awkward situation into something entertaining. If there was a meter that measured the popularity of mimes in this world, it definitively moved up a few notches. They were a hit and would definitely get noticed; maybe even a YouTube video of their performance would surface later.

Frances breathed a sigh of relief. She had been nervous all night about agreeing to the pantomime. As her head hit the pillow that night, she was pleased that it had turned out better than she thought. "That went well," she whispered as she fell asleep.

– Ten –
Another Complication

LISA MORENO WALKED THE FOUR BLOCKS from her small apartment to Fort Lauderdale Beach nearly every morning before she started her day. Her shiny brown, shoulder-length hair fell perfectly on either side of her face. Her perfectly behaved hair, her cute as a button nose, and her wide smile were the first things people noticed about Lisa. As she stood on the beach, she wiggled her toes in the cool sand, watching the lifeguard cart pass by, making tire tracks on the pristine beach.

She called, "Good morning" to the lifeguard that was putting up umbrellas and beach chairs. He waved, smiled, and returned her good morning. Since moving to the area, she could not get enough of the friendliness shown by people in the South. She thought he must be a new lifeguard since she recognized the regulars. He was tan and good-looking, as lifeguards are apt to be, but this one was too young and too muscular for her tastes.

She had put her love life on hold to pursue her dream of starting a catering business. Still, a girl on a tropical beach who has recently lost ten pounds can't help but daydream about romance, and that was what Lisa was doing this morning. She had come close to marriage once, but the groom got cold feet thinking of the commitment involved and left town, leaving her alone and a little bitter towards relationships.

She first set foot on this beach five years ago while attending a girlfriend's wedding. She made herself a promise to return. She was so drawn to this tropical paradise that she set a goal to quit her job at her family's Italian restaurant in New Jersey and move to Florida. Not being a risk-taker, she was proud of herself for taking such a bold step. She never went to college or received formal training, but she felt she had the stuff to run a top-notch catering business. Of course, sometimes she was nervous that it would not work out and that she would have to return home or get another job or many other scenarios that sometimes kept her up at night. But, as she frequently reminded herself, what a place to try and fail.

The blue-green water, which looked almost fake through the lens of her polarized sunglasses, was calmly lapping the shore. As she gazed at the sunrise, she wondered why she loved the beach so much. It seemed to have healing and restorative powers over her. Why did people in general love the being near the water? Why did they fantasize about tropical vacations on a sunny beach? She did not know why, and she did not have time to contemplate. She had to get to work. She did a few yoga poses, took a few deep breaths, and then headed to her shared kitchen space to begin her day. As she sat in her small office, which consisted of a file cabinet, a card table and a chair, her assistant, Tasha, walked in and greeted her.

The peaceful feelings from watching the sunrise slowly faded and Lisa switched to business owner mode. Not taking time for small talk with her employee, she got right to her instructions. "When the extra help arrives, I need you to take the lead and get them started on the food prep for the Birnam wedding. Let's go over my notes before they get here." Lisa was very organized but not very technically oriented. Her system of keeping track of her catering process just looked messy. While covering the critical details with Tasha, she was shuffling and dropping pages from a large a stack of paper covered with handwritten notes underscored with scribbles, circles, and stars.

"Lisa, how long will you resist technology? Why don't you type the menus and schedules on your computer?" asked Tasha. "It would be so much easier."

"I have told you before. I am a visual person so I like to put pen to paper to see my ideas. That is just the way I work. If you want to open a catering business and type things on the computer, go right ahead," said Lisa.

Although Tasha could not comprehend a person that was so separated from technology, she could not argue with Lisa's success so, once again, she dropped the topic.

Lisa continued, "Make sure you check the sous chef's work today and ensure that the quality of the cutting, slicing, and dicing is consistent. If we do our best work and make a good impression this weekend, we could be busy doing large society weddings for years to come."

Tasha assured her, "Got it. I will make sure everything

is perfect. By the way, I never asked how you landed such a big wedding."

"My friend Frances is the bride's aunt. I met her a long time ago, before I moved to Florida. Frances made the introduction, but I made a real connection with the bride and her mother. They loved my ideas and my food so they hired me at the first meeting." Lisa's smile faded and she spoke with annoyance. "Where is Luis? He should be here by now."

"Don't be so irritable. You told Luis to go by the warehouse and get more supplies this morning before he came to work. You have to relax. Everything is under control. Did you do your yoga this morning?"

"Yes, I did my yoga. This is just so important to me that I can't help but be stressed out. I'm sorry I'm snapping at you but the snapping is most likely to continue today. I'm just warning you."

"I understand," said Tasha. "Snap away. I won't hold it against you."

Lisa's only other employee, Luis, was a recent hire that showed great potential. He was a young man that decided what he wanted to do very soon after his high school graduation. He tried to attend classes at the community college, but it was not right for him. He loved food, people, and parties, so working in a catering business was a good fit. Luis walked into the kitchen with a box of trays under one arm and a piece of paper in his hand. He handed the paper to Lisa and said, "Look at this! Do you know about this?"

Examining it quickly, Lisa handed it back and said, "Why are you handing me a protest flyer?"

Luis said in an exasperated voice, "Look at the date and place! It is an all-day bike rally on Saturday. They will probably be riding on the trail in front of the museum as wedding guests are arriving!"

Lisa grabbed the flyer back. One line on at the bottom caught her eye and made her panic. It said "plenty of parking at the museum." She knew the protesters would block not only her entrance to the venue, but all the other wedding vendors. While she agreed that people had a right to peacefully protest and express their point of view, she was really angry at being thrown this complication. "Where did you get this?" she asked.

"A friend of mine works at the Under Grounds coffee shop and they put these flyers up this morning. What are we going to do? This is a disaster!" said Luis.

"Don't panic, Luis!" said Tasha. "Let's think of a solution, not dwell on the problem." Quickly looking up the website listed on the flyer, Tasha saw that a guy named Lance was the protest organizer.

Lisa gave them quick instructions. "Tasha, you and Luis try to reach out to this guy Lance and see if they will move the starting point of the protest to another place or reschedule it or something. I will call the bride's mother and let her know what is going on."

Tasha took Luis into the back of the kitchen to scold him. She said in a whispered shout, "Lisa is under a lot of pressure with this wedding. It is very important to her. Stop acting like a moody teenager and overreacting. What is wrong with you?"

"This wedding is really important to me too," he said, calming down.

"What? Why is it so important to you?"

"I want to make a good impression on the bride. I used to know her in high school and I don't want to look like an idiot."

"You are friends with the bride? Why didn't you say so?"

"Well, we are not exactly good friends. I'm not sure if she will even remember me. We had several classes together in high school but we didn't exactly hang out." Luis could remember his first and only conversation with Ella like it was yesterday. They both stood at the dry erase board working algebra problems to review for the final exam. Ella observed his work and complimented him on his neat handwriting and how quickly he factored numbers. Those affirming words from this beautiful girl set him on his first career path to major in accounting.

Tasha said, "Oh, so you mean she was popular and you weren't. Am I right?"

"Basically, yes. But high school was yesterday and this is today."

Showing more tenderness toward her coworker, Tasha said, "Well don't worry about what a girl you used to know in high school thinks about you. You are a good at what you do and you should be proud." And injecting a bit of reality into the situation as she was prone to do, she added, "Anyway, the bride will be busy during the wedding and won't have much time to catch up on high school memories with a member of the catering staff. Am I right?"

Tasha was wrong in saying that Luis should not worry about it. He would worry about it. What Ella Birnam thought of him should be of no consequence, but in fact it was very important to him. Ella was Luis's first high school crush, and he would never forget her. Some people have a hard time moving past their high school identities, and Luis was one of those people. In his mind, if he could somehow get Ella's validation, he could move forward with his life to bigger and better things.

"I know she will be busy, but I still want to impress her. Is that so wrong?" he said. Then he added, "One more thing. Can you act like you work for me during the reception? I want her to think I own the business."

Tasha summed up her answer and ended this conversation in one definite word, "Not!"

The poet Robert Browning said, "God's in His heaven – All's right with the world." That is the way Deidre felt on Friday morning, although she did not know enough of English poets or of God to express it that way. She was full of peace and good feelings about the wedding. The bridal brunch had just ended, and some family members lingered at the table as the bride and bridesmaids filed out of The Circle dining room. Deidre's peaceful feeling came to an abrupt end when her phone rang and the caterer, Lisa Moreno, gave her the news about the protest and the potential conflict with the wedding.

Family members recognized Deidre's facial expression and posture change from blissfully relaxed to agonizing worry in a few seconds. They waited patiently to see what news had caused this metamorphosis. As soon as her daughter was out of sight, Deidre spilled. "This is terrible! I don't know what to do. This is awful! Why do they have to protest? Why on a Saturday? Why can't they just let people do what they want? I don't know what to do!"

Lady said, "Deidre, calm down. What are you babbling about? What has happened? Who was on the phone?"

Deidra answered, "That was the caterer, Lisa. She found out that there is a bicycle protest rally Saturday and it begins and ends at the Flagler Museum."

Thomas asked, "What do they have against bicycles? It is a very enjoyable form of exercise. I was thinking about biking more often now that the weather is cooler. People are against the silliest things these days."

Deidre continued, "It is an all-day protest and they may still be there when the wedding begins. What should we do? How do we fix this?"

Freddie squirmed in his chair, thinking that protest sounded vaguely familiar. "That's funny," he said. "My ex-stepson Lance was telling me his group was planning a protest. I had no idea it was the same day as the wedding. Funny coincidence, isn't it?" Trying to interject some humor into the situation he added, "Maybe he is sore at not being invited to the wedding."

Alexandra checked the local protest website and pulled up the page. She confirmed that Lance was the organizer.

"Freddie!" shouted Deidre. "You have to convince Lance to call it off."

"I don't think he will do that," said Freddie.

"Why not?" she asked.

"Well, he tried to get twenty-five thousand bucks out of me last night at his birthday party. I dodged the issue and escaped the party with my wallet intact and have been ignoring his texts since. I don't think he is in the mood to do me any favors."

Deidre implored, "Freddie, I beg you. Just tell him you will give him the money if he calls off the protest."

Lady added, "He will do it. That boy is motivated by money. Pay him off, Freddie."

"The problem, dear sisters, is that I do not have that kind of cash available to me right now."

As they pondered this new complication threatening the wedding, they all instinctively turned to Frances, who was sipping her coffee and thinking. Deidre turned toward her and implored, "Frances what do you think we should do?"

"Well, based on what you have told us, and what Freddie said about Lance, I think I have a plan that will make everyone happy and solve this problem."

"Well tell us!" Deidre said.

"I would rather not involve everyone. Lady, Alexandra, Freddie, and I will handle it. We will go to my room after breakfast and strategize." Turning to Deidre and clasping her hand, she said, "Don't worry, between the four of us, we will solve this problem. You concentrate on the final details of the wedding and leave this protest problem to us."

Deidre exhaled and felt the feeling of relief flood over her again. It did not last. As soon as Frances finished her sentence, Deidre's phone chimed. She looked at the text message and was horrified. Her emotions ramped up again and she screamed in a voice that traveled up and down the hotel loggia. "Oh no! Oh no! I just got a text from the minister. He is very sick and does not think he will recover in time for the wedding. What are we going to do? How will I find an official on such short notice? Why are so many bad things happening at the last minute? Do you think it is some sort of omen or sign that Ella and Auden should not get married?"

Frances was the only one that attempted to answer to Deidre's philosophical question. She said, "Don't be silly. These are not omens or signs; they are just complications. So many things go wrong with a big event like this. People are not perfect and things just go wrong. Let's not panic. I'm am sure we can put our heads together and come up with a solution to this problem too."

Alexandra, who had been quiet up to this point, asked, "Does the minister have a backup? Sometimes they have more than one person that does weddings? Call him and ask?"

Deidre started to breathe again. "Of course! What a great idea. You are a wonderful child. I will call him right now." Deidre rushed out into the loggia with her phone to call the minister. Within ten minutes she returned with an almost angelic look on her face. She said, "You will never believe what just happened. It was so serendipitous."

All eyes were on her as they waited for the amazing story to be told. She continued, adding a dramatic tone to her voice. "I called the minister and he said he did not have a backup and so I hung up and started to cry. Just then a woman walked up to me and asked if I was all right. She said she recognized me from high school. I guess I really have not changed that much. Of course, I didn't recognize her but you will never guess what she said next. You will never guess what she does for a living."

Lady, who loved guessing games, said, "She overheard your phone call. The whole hotel heard your frantic phone call. She is a minister of some kind and she said she will be happy to officiate the wedding tomorrow."

Deidre was annoyed with her sister for stealing the thunder to her unbelievable story by stating exactly what had transpired in the lobby. However, she was so happy that she decided not to let it bother her this time. She admitted, "Yes! That is exactly what happened. I think the universe knew what I needed and sent her to me."

Frances asked, "What is her name? Maybe Lady remembers her from high school."

"She introduced herself as Ministrix Beatrix," said Deidre. "And she gave me her card."

Thomas, who had been listening on and off to this conversation, finally chimed in, "What were her parents thinking? Why would they name their child Ministrix with a last name like Beatrix? Parents can be so thoughtless. I bet she was made fun of at school for her odd sounding name. You know how children can be cruel. I remember several nicknames they gave me like —"

Lady stopped her brother from another ramble. "Her name is not 'Ministrix.' That is her title. It is sometimes used as the feminine version of Minister. Her first name is Beatrix. I think it is kind of catchy and easy to remember. I wonder what her last name is. I don't remember a Beatrix in high school."

Deidre said, "Well I don't care about her name or title or if we remember her from high school. She seems like a lovely person and I'm glad she is available to do the wedding. It is a good sign." Looking at her watch she said, "I have to go now and be with Ella. I'll see you all later at the family reception."

The family members dispersed, and the recently deputized problem solvers followed Frances to her room. Alexandra was exhilarated at being included in the meeting and wondered what her aunt had in mind to solve the latest crisis. She thought that coming to the wedding weekend a few days early and hanging around older people would be boring. She could not have been more mistaken.

After closing the door, Freddie plopped down on the loveseat next to the window, curious as to what this wonder woman would suggest. "Well, Frances," he said. "What do you have in mind and why the secret meeting behind closed doors?"

Frances explained, "The fewer people that know about this the better. You know Deidre is overwhelmed and quick problem solving is too taxing on Thomas' brain. It's better if this stays between us and we handle it." Frances paused, not sure where to begin. "Freddie, you say Susan changed the locks on the beach house in Boca?"

"Yes," said Freddie slowly, wondering how this related to the problem at hand.

"And, you say that the house is technically still in your name?"

"Yes," he said, again wondering why property ownership was relevant.

Frances asked, "Are you familiar with the alarm system at the house?"

"Well ..." said Freddie, feeling a little sick to his stomach at what Frances might be suggesting.

Frances revealed the plan. "Here is my idea. We will break into the beach house that you technically own and retrieve the expensive watches that already belong to you. You will take them to an all-night pawnshop downtown and get the cash to pay off Lance. He will be so happy to get the money, he will willingly call off the protest."

Lady said, "You are suggesting breaking, entering, and stealing as the solution? You are mad as a hatter."

Alexandra looked at Lady for explanation. "What is a hatter?"

Lady explained, "Hat-makers in the old days used mercury to stiffen the brim but the mercury caused brain damage and some of them went crazy. But that is not important right now."

"It is not breaking and entering if you own the property. And it is not stealing if you take what is rightfully yours," said Frances, justifying her plan that was completely legal, although she knew it sounded a little crazy.

Freddie was a little stunned at Frances's suggestion, but as he thought about it, the idea started to grow on him. Yes, the house was technically still his. Yes, the watches did belong to him. He could do whatever he wanted in his house with his watches. A feeling of empowerment came over him and he said, "I'll do it! I will do it just to see Susan's reaction when she finds out. I think I will even leave a note saying 'Dear Susan, who is a mature adult now?'" He thought for a moment, "Oh, hang on. She will probably be at the beach house this weekend. And worse yet, even if she is out her dogs will be there."

"I'm surprised at you. You are afraid of a few Pekingese dogs?" Lady asked.

"You don't know the power of the Peke," said Freddie putting his sandaled foot on the coffee table and pointing out the tiny scars on his ankles. "They have never liked me and have left marks on my ankles to prove it. Also their shrill, yapping bark will alert the neighbors."

Frances added, "Never mind about the dogs. That is

a minor problem. We need to find out when Susan will be away from the house."

"I've got it," said Freddie. "I will call Lance and tell him that I will give him the money if he calls off the protest. He will be so thrilled to get the money that he will gladly answer questions about his mother's schedule. I bet he can also give me the new alarm codes to the house. This is perfect. Frances, I think this is going to work. I have not been this excited about a Friday night in a long time."

"Why don't you just ask Lance to go to the beach house and get the watches for you?" asked Alexandra.

"Lance is a nice kid, but not very bright. He might come back with a rolling pin rather than a Rolex. Or he might keep the watches for himself and say he couldn't find them. No, I think we should do it," said Freddie. He stepped out onto the hotel balcony to make the call to Lance.

Alexandra watched him through the glass, trying to read his body language. By his movements, she gathered that the conversation was going well. Thinking through the plan in her head, she asked her aunts, "What do we wear to a break-in?"

Frances responded, "We will wear all black so we are not noticeable at night. Did you bring any black outfits?"

"Yes," Alexandra proudly responded. "I have black leggings and a black tee shirt and black tennis shoes."

Lady pouted. "I did not bring any black. I did not think I would need black for an October wedding in

Palm Beach. I will have to wear light gray. I hate not being prepared."

Freddie stepped back into the room from the balcony with a smug smile on his face. "I knew I could count on Lance to put aside his social concerns for cold hard cash. I told him I would give him ten thousand to call off the protest. He countered with fifteen and we settled on twelve five. I like a man that can negotiate. I think he learned that from me," Freddie said proudly. "I also got it out of Lance that the beach house is empty this weekend; Susan went out of town today and Lance is staying with a friend. He says he usually walks the dogs before sunset."

Thinking of possible pitfalls, Alexandra asked, "What if Susan calls the police or wants the watches back?"

Freddie was confident Susan would listen to reason. He assured them, "I will tell her that I was in the neighborhood, stopped by the house, took the watches, sold them, and gave the money to Lance for his cause. How can she be upset with that? I will look like the world's greatest ex-husband and ex-stepfather. Not that there is such a competition currently, but if there were, I would win. Should we call Deidre and give her the good news? Poor thing is probably frazzled with worry."

"No, not yet," said Frances. "Let's wait until we have the watches in hand before calling her."

Lady added, "Yes, we don't want to get her hopes up yet. So much could go wrong with this plan."

"Don't throw a wet blanket on it, Lady," said Freddie. "I think our plan is airtight except, there is one more thing. We need to bring some meat." They all looked at him, puzzled. "For the Pekes," he explained.

"We can get some dog treats on the way," said Lady.

"No, it has to be meat. Susan's dogs are fussy about different brands of dog treats. She would disagree with me but all her dogs love raw meat. I used to secretly give them meat scraps from my plate. Susan would kill me if she knew," said Freddie with a satisfied chuckle.

"You mean meat like a steak?" said Alexandra.

"We could get stew meat," added Lady. "It is buy one get one free this week at Publix."

"All right, we will stop by Publix on the way and get stew meat," said Frances.

"We will meet in the lobby at ten o'clock tonight following the rehearsal dinner."

– Eleven –
Thomas finds Maria

THOMAS FRIDAY WENT BACK TO HIS ROOM for a post breakfast nap. He had a restless night's sleep following his visit to the Morikami Gardens. He could not stop thinking about Maria. Thomas was not blessed with a brain that was prone to deep reflection, but for the first time in a long time his brain was getting a workout in that department. He could not understand why Maria had made such an impression on him.

He had not known many women intimately. He did not date in high school aside from the obligatory homecoming and prom dates. He met and married his first wife in college, and his second wife practically proposed to him. He enjoyed a warm brotherly relationship with his sisters as long as he stayed out of their way and did not make them unhappy. But on the whole, women were a mystery to him.

What motivated this woman who worked long hours to help her family, who gave up her dreams and yet seemed content? He thought that Maria was unlike the women he was used to being around, except perhaps Frances. He could see Frances and Maria being friends, and he made a mental note to tell Frances more about her.

His attempt at a nap was unsuccessful. Tossing and turning in bed a few more times, he decided to get up and get another coffee downstairs. As he was waiting for the elevator to return to his room, he spied a rare Oncidium Sharry Baby orchid in a beautiful tropical arrangement placed on an antique chest in between the elevators. Even though there was a crowd waiting for the elevator, Thomas stepped forward through the crowd toward the flower arrangement and sniffed a long, loud sniff. As he stepped back, all eyes were on him and he felt an explanation was necessary. "It smells, like chocolate. The Oncidium Sharry Baby orchid has a wonderful chocolate smell. Some people say it smells like vanilla or dark chocolate, but this one smells like milk chocolate," he said, pointing to the arrangement and stepping aside so others could follow his example.

As is the case with most modern Americans, they rarely stop and smell the flowers, and so no one stepped forward and no one said anything. They just stared at him with blank faces as they continued to wait. Thomas concluded this awkward show in front of the crowd by saying, "It is really quite remarkable. It is a special kind of orchid that smells like chocolate." He decided to let the others step ahead of him onto the elevator, and he said to the crowd as the doors closed, "I will catch the next one."

As the elevator closed, an idea came to him like a bolt of lightning. He would go to the local garden store, buy Maria an Oncidium Sharry Baby orchid and deliver it to the nursing home where she worked with a note.

The more he thought about this idea, the more excited he became. Within twenty minutes of having his brilliant idea, Thomas was in the garden section of the local home improvement store. He was in luck; they had a nice example of the sweet-smelling orchid in a decorative pot. He put the pot under his arm and started to walk toward the cashier. The sight of rows and rows of colorful flowers caused him to stop and stare as if he were in a trance. There were yellow snapdragons, pink periwinkle, blue salvia, red pentas, multi-color petunias, and many other beautiful flowers. On and on the rows went like a beautiful impressionist painting.

Viewing so many beautiful flowers at once almost paralyzed him. He tried to walk but something was keeping him in his tracks. He looked back to see the pocket on his cargo pants was caught on the display shelf. He tugged and tugged and pulled his leg forward with force, trying to free himself. He did free himself and the momentum caused him to land chest-first on the palettes of freshly watered flowers. The containers holding the annuals were not meant to hold the weight of a middle-aged man so they gave way and Thomas, along with the flowers, slid to the floor, scraping his knees and his right elbow on the pavement. The orchid arrangement however, due to Thomas's early football training, was securely tucked under his left arm and completely intact.

The salesclerk wearing an orange apron stopped spraying the flowers, walked over, looked down at Thomas, and said, "Can I help you sir?"

Thomas, still in a jumbled pile on the ground, held up the orchid arrangement and said, "I'll take this one."

There is a type of elder-care facility, ubiquitous in Florida, called an adult congregate living facility or better known to Floridians as an ACLF. The Friday family fortune was made in developing and managing ACLFs on both the west and east coast of Florida. These facilities are categorized in levels much like hotels from luxury to affordable. There are first-class facilities that provide spacious rooms and a full range of services to their residents at surprisingly exorbitant prices for those who can afford it. There are also many less expensive options, with varying levels of amenities and services for families that are not rolling in the dough. And then there are a few facilities that would make a good script for a horror film where you would not want your worst enemy to live. But that is a subject for another book.

Maria worked at a medium-priced, well-run religious facility called Saintly Shores and had placed her grandparents there, taking advantage of the employee discounted rate. Saintly Shores happened to be one of the Friday family's newest acquisitions. They completely remolded and rebranded it. Max oversaw the construction, Deidre helped hire the staff, and Freddie marketed the facility. The name contained the word "shores" because Freddie said if you were on the third floor facing east and stood on one foot and leaned out the window and looked around the building, you could see a glimpse of the Atlantic Ocean. It was appropriately named "saintly" because of the compassionate staff that looked after the residents.

Doris, the head nurse, was that rare breed of person who did her job with excellence no matter if she was praised or rewarded. Doris carefully hired and trained each nurse to make sure that the residents were comfortable and well looked after. She ran a tight ship and would check and recheck to make sure that the defenseless elderly under her care were not neglected. She trained her nurses and staff accordingly and would not hesitate to fire anyone who did not do their job with excellence. In addition, she knew each resident by name, their particular physical or mental disability and how to handle each one so that things ran smoothly.

Doris had worked the night shift and was giving her final instructions to the nurse on duty at the front desk. "Mr. Saunders has wandered off again early this morning," she informed the front desk nurse. "He was working in the garden out back at four o'clock this morning. I let him stay out there for a while and then I lost track of him. He is probably next-door at the garden shop. The shop owners are familiar with his condition, so they don't mind."

The front desk nurse asked, "Why does he have to be around plants all the time?"

Doris knew his biography well from having spent time with him. She answered, "Mr. Saunders used to work in the landscaping department at Disney World. He spent over twenty years tending the flowerbeds at the theme parks in the early morning hours when the parks were closed. I don't think he could ever switch his internal time clock back to normal after he retired. He feels most comfortable digging through the flowerbeds in the middle of the night, so we let him."

She continued the instructions, "When he comes in the front door this morning, he will probably have a plant in his hand. He often steals plants from the store next door or digs up the neighbor's flowers. He can't help it; he does not know what he is doing. When he walks in, just take the plant from him and guide him back to his room. He will be all dirty and disheveled so you will need to call David to help him take a shower before he goes to bed. Then ask one of the staff to return the plant to the store."

The front desk nurse accepted her assignment with zeal. She had been on the job only two days and was eager to make a good impression on Doris. She would successfully corral Mr. Saunders as soon as he came through the doors.

As Doris pulled out of the parking lot, Thomas Friday pulled in. The name Saintly Shores was vaguely familiar to him, and he wondered if this was one of his family's properties. Thomas ran the west coast branch of the family business, so was not familiar with the recent acquisitions on the east coast.

After his little accident at the garden center, he considered going back to the hotel and changing, but he did not want to delay seeing Maria. He entered the automatic sliding doors with black dirt smeared on his shirt and holes torn in his pants. His elbow was still bleeding, and blood was seeping through his pants, forming dark circles below his knees. The front desk nurse smiled a wide smile and said, "Well, good morning, Mr. Saunders."

Thomas was a little confused and looked behind him to see if he had walked in with a man named Saunders. Seeing no one, he explained. "No, I am here to see Maria. I brought this flower for her and I wondered if I could see her."

"Of course you can, Mr. Saunders," said the nurse trying to extricate the flower from under his arm. "You can come along with me to your room and after David has helped you get these dirty clothes off, and showered, we will tell Maria that you want to see her."

"No, you don't understand. I am not Mr. Saunders. I don't live here."

The nurse did not budge. She grabbed Thomas's arm firmly and started to pull him back through the double doors to the resident wing.

"No wait, I just want to see Maria," Thomas said as he dug his heels into the area rug in the reception area. "You don't understand. I don't live here."

"Mr. Saunders, don't be difficult. Come along. Let me take the plant and I will water it and put it in the dining hall and you can enjoy it later."

"Water it!" said Thomas, outraged. "You don't water orchids! You mist them. You might kill it. It needs special care and only Maria should take care of it."

Seeing this was going to be a difficult situation, the nurse pushed the buzzer and said, "I will call David and he can help you back to your room."

Thomas was indignant. He did not look a day over forty-five and this woman was mistaking him for a resident. Thomas said, "What is your name? I am going to report you to your superior. I think my family owns this facility and if you don't let me go and call Maria, I am going to have you fired."

"Okay, Mr. Saunders. I will let the President of the United States and the Queen of England know you are unhappy," said the nurse, getting impatient with his delusions of grandeur. The head nurse had trained them not to argue with the patients but to enter their delusional world with good humor and a sweet voice. This nurse still needed practice, as she seemed to infuriate Thomas all the more.

David, a robust male nurse, walked through the double doors and put both arms around Thomas's shoulders. He too was a new employee and had never seen Mr. Saunders in action, so assumed Thomas was the difficult patient. He fought with Thomas for a while trying to get him through the doors and back to his room. Thomas's bleeding body worried David and he wondered what other injuries he had sustained during his all-night adventure. He finally poked him with a syringe, giving him a mild sedative that he had brought in his pocket for such situations.

Thomas shouted, "Ouch!" Then he shouted louder, "Maria, Maria, Maria," until his voice died away to a faint moan. "Maria," he said one more time for good measure before he passed out still clutching the flower arrangement tightly.

Maria was in a nearby room helping a patient when she heard her name being shouted. She rushed to the lobby and was shocked to see Thomas. "Why did you give Mr. Friday a sedative?" she said with alarm. "What were you thinking?"

Doris was walking back in the front door, having been summoned back for this emergency. Overhearing Maria's panicked question, she asked, "Why did you call him Mr. Friday?"

When he woke up, Thomas was reclined in a hospital-type bed. Doris, the front desk nurse, and David looked at him with mixture of grave concern and fear. Maria was seated by the bed and was smiling at Thomas almost to the point of laughter. Doris spoke first, "Mr. Friday, I want you to know how sorry we all are for the terrible, terrible mistake we made today. I hope you can understand the confusion and accept our sincere apology for mistaking you for our resident Mr. Saunders. I understand your family is the ownership group of this facility. We hope you can overlook our error and be assured it will not happen again."

The sedative had not taken the edge off Thomas's anger. He was still irritated. He blurted out, "All of you out of the room except Maria or I will have you all fired. And where is my plant?"

Once they were alone, Maria asked, "How did you find me?"

Thomas explained, "You said you worked at a facility next to a garden center. I am pretty good at finding garden centers." Considering all that had transpired that morning and deciding to skip the small talk portion of their conversation, Thomas asked her, "Would you like to come to my niece's wedding tomorrow as my guest? I know I am a little older than you and I was just divorced less than a year ago, but I really enjoy your company. I promise it won't be boring and there will be lots of beautiful flowers."

"I would like that, Thomas. I need to ask for the day off but, somehow, I think the head nurse will give it to me. And by the way, thank you for the lovely Oncidium orchid. I put it on my desk while you were passed out."

"It smells like chocolate," said Thomas with a dreamy smile on his face.

– Twelve –
Meet the Family

FLORIDA WAS PREPARING AN IMPRESSIVE WEEKEND
for the Birnam-Woods wedding. The salty ocean waves,
the balmy breeze, the waving palm fronds, and the sun
shining in the bright blue sky worked in concert to welcome guests arriving at The Breakers. It was Friday afternoon and family members and friends were checking
into the hotel in anticipation of the happy event to take
place the following day. A typical destination wedding
will include a welcome reception for the families and
close friends, a wedding rehearsal followed by a dinner,
the wedding ceremony, a post-wedding breakfast, and
possibly an excursion. The Birnam-Woods wedding was
at the welcome reception stage.

Deidre enlisted her family to mill around the reception and make sure the members of the Woods clan were
properly welcomed. Freddie was the first to arrive in the
courtyard, followed by Alexandra. She greeted her uncle
with enthusiasm and said, "Uncle Freddie, I can't stop
thinking about the break-in tonight. I'm so excited to be
committing a crime and yet not committing a crime. You
know what I mean?"

"Shhhh," said Freddie putting his index finger to his lips. Leaning in, he joked, "You don't want the Woodses to think … I mean the Woodens. How do you say the plural of Woods? Anyway, we don't want the Woods family to know we are planning a jewelry heist."

Freddie looked admiringly at his niece, "You look lovely, Alexandra. Did you get that dress while shopping with your aunts?" Alexandra nodded. She was wearing a pale blue dress and her mother's diamond necklace. Her cheeks and arms were gaining color from the sun. She was beginning to look like a Floridian again and that made her happy. Freddie, almost reading her mind said, "You are looking more like a Florida-Friday each day."

Frances and Lady arrived in the courtyard and joined Freddie and Alexandra. Frances pulled out her phone to read a text from Deidre. "Deidre says Ella and the brides-maids are still getting ready and running late so we are to cover for them until they get here. She has assigned each of us members of the Woods family to talk to. Freddie, you are supposed to charm Auden's grandmother. Her name is Ethel. It will take some work to make her like this family and you are the man for the job. Alexandra, you introduce yourself to Auden's cousins and basically anyone under twenty-five. Lady, you talk to Auden's dad. When Thomas gets here, he can talk to Auden's Aunt Trudy. I will continue to smooth things over with Auden's mother. We are going to be their best friends by the end of the night. Got it?"

"Oh great," complained Freddie. "Thomas gets to talk to a young woman and I get Grandma Ethel. No worries, team. I will have her onboard by the end of the evening. Old women love me. There is not a woman in our ACLFs on this coast who does not know the name Freddie Friday."

Lady said, "Don't complain, Freddie. I watch *Downton Abbey* and read British mystery novels and I have to make conversation with a NASCAR and NFL fan."

Alexandra pleaded with her aunt as she looked at the Woods' many young cousins filing into the room. "You want me to just go up and talk to them? I don't know what to say to them. They don't know who I am. They will think I'm weird."

Frances gave her young niece a sympathetic look. She knew Alexandra was naturally shy and needed a little push. She enlisted help. "Freddie, you are a master at mingling. Give Alexandra some tips to get her started."

Freddie quickly called to his memory things that had become second nature to him from years of experience as a salesman. He felt he could have taught a six-week course on mingling but gave Alexandra enough to get her started. "There are a few ways you can start a conversation. After you introduce yourself you can make an observation about the hotel, the food, or the weather. Or you can compliment them on something they are wearing—always stay positive. Don't ask yes or no questions and never take out your phone. Whatever you do, don't ask personal questions right off the bat. Also, don't say anything derogatory about the other guests. Remember, they are just as nervous as you are."

Obediently Alexandra bravely walked toward her

conversational assignment. Her head was spinning with Freddie's rapid-fire mingling tips.

Freddie sidled up to an elderly woman at the bar and struck up a conversation. "You must be Auden's grandmother I've heard so much about," Freddie said, stretching the truth a little. "I am Ella's Uncle Freddie. Nice to meet you."

"I did not know Ella had an Uncle Freddie," said Grandma Ethel, sounding unimpressed.

"Yes, I'm her uncle. I have been for years. I'm surprised she didn't mention me. Well anyway, here we are. Welcome to Palm Beach. I live here but I understand you all come from North Florida. How was your drive? Have you ever been to The Breakers before? It's a magnificent hotel isn't it?"

Auden's grandmother was wondering if this man would ever stop talking so she could answer at least one of his many questions. Not being a chatty conversationalist and wanting to get her point across, Grandma Ethel said, "We are from the Gainesville area. The drive was long and I have never been to The Breakers." Ethel had lived in Florida all her life but had never been to The Breakers because, although she could afford it, she didn't want people to think she was puttin' on airs or acting any better than she ought to.

She had lived through the depression, and she often reminded people of that when she felt they were excessive in their materialistic consumption. Although attending the wedding cost her nothing, she was looking forward with secret delight to the many opportunities to point out unnecessary spending and obvious excess at her grandson's wedding. One of those opportunities came in her conversation with Freddie. "In my day, young man, weddings were simple. I don't think you have to spend all this money and have a big fancy wedding to just get hitched."

"I couldn't agree with you more, Ethel. I have been married three times and I can tell you, the money spent was not worth it," said Freddie, with wisdom that comes from experience.

Grandma Ethel was shocked at Freddie's statement and could not help but raise her voice. "You have been married three times?"

There was an awkward silence in the room following Ethel's exclamation and everyone stared in Freddie's direction. He smiled at the crowd and then, in two beats, the conversations resumed again.

"What is your problem, young man? Why can't you stay married?" questioned Ethel.

Freddie was delighted that she called him young. Confiding in this old soul, he said, "I don't know, Ethel. I have been trying to figure that out for some time. Women seem to like me at first but then shove me out the door. Sometimes I don't last as long as a pair of their running shoes. I think I like the idea of marriage but when it comes to living with the flesh-and-blood woman on a day-to-day basis, that's where I have the trouble." Trying to be positive and remembering Lady's suggestion about not droning on about his marital troubles, Freddie said, "I bet you were a beautiful bride, Ethel. Do you have a picture?"

Ethel did have a picture in her handbag. She intended to show it to Ella and point out that her dress was white and that her neighbor helped her make it for only twenty dollars. Of course she would not adjust that number for inflation, making her point more dramatic. She would also point out that she was married for over fifty years before her dear husband passed, so she must have done something right. She handed the faded photo to Freddie.

He examined it and said honestly, "You were a looker, Ethel. I bet you had to fight them off with a stick when you were a young girl."

Freddie was winning this woman's heart. No matter how old or wrinkled or jaded a woman may become, she always likes the attention of an attractive young man praising her qualities. She thought that if Freddie was any indication of the Friday family personality, she would enjoy this weekend.

"Freddie," Ethel said, "Have you met my youngest daughter, Auden's Aunt Trudy?"

"Trudy? No I have not met her. Is she in the room?" said Freddie scanning the courtyard.

"Yes, she is over there," said Ethel pointing to a woman in conversation with Lady and Thomas.

"Trudy is a very successful businesswoman. She started her own goat farm and is doing very well selling goat cheese to grocers all over the South," said Grandma Ethel with pride.

Freddie spotted Trudy Woods. She was a tall woman that was very tan and very fit. She had the appearance of a woman that spent most of her time outdoors. Her short dress showed off her well-developed leg muscles. The word beautiful did not come to Freddie's mind. His first impression of Trudy was that she would compete well if thrown into a mixed martial arts cage. And yet, as he looked at her, he decided that she was not unattractive.

Ethel continued the biography of her daughter, "Trudy has never married. She is so dedicated to her goat farm. It will take a special man to persuade her to marry. You should introduce yourself."

Freddie looked at Ethel, wondering if he was being set up with a goat herder or if Ethel was just being polite. He said, "I think I will go introduce myself now." Downing his drink, he parted, saying, "Ethel, you owe me a dance at the wedding."

Freddie scored the approval of Grandma Ethel and was off to win Auden's Aunt Trudy over to team Friday. He approached Lady, Thomas, and Trudy and joined their conversation. Lady introduced him, "Trudy, this is my brother, Ella's uncle, Freddie."

Trudy held out a hand and said in a jocular tone, "Glad to know you, Freddie."

Freddie shook her strong, well-tanned hand and said, "I understand you are a goat herder, Trudy."

"I don't really herd them. They are free-range goats. I raise them and make goat cheese out of their milk."

"How fascinating," said Freddie, not sure where to go with a conversation about goats. Then he remembered a recent conversation and said, "Do you ever do yoga with your goats? I hear that is all the rage. A friend of mine drives an hour to a goat farm to do yoga while baby goats vault off her back and generally frolic around. It sounds exotic to me but—to each his own. I told my friend I would help her rebrand her business as "Goat-ga" or "Yoat-ga" but she did not go for it. There is such potential combining those two words."

Lady smiled politely at her brother's attempt at humor and Thomas looked confused. But Trudy guffawed and slapped Freddie on the back, causing his drink to slosh out of the cup and onto the floor. She repeated, "Goat-ga, I like that. I like a good pun, Freddie. I will have to look into goat yoga. If I can make money off the idea, I will try anything. Yoat-ga! That is funny."

Realizing he was entertaining this woman, Freddie continued. "Yes, at the end of every yoga class you could say 'Na-maaaaa-ste.'" Once again he was smacked on the back by Trudy's right hand in reward for his quick wit. This time he felt his feet rise off the ground at the point of impact. Freddie's conversation with Trudy continued along amiable lines.

As he was getting to know this woman, he could not help but think how she was completely different from the women he usually interacted with, and he was actually at ease and enjoying himself. It was almost uncanny how every good quality that Trudy exhibited reminded him of a contrasting irritating quality in his ex-wives. When Freddie made a joke, his ex-wives were apt to roll their eyes and tell him not to be such a smart-aleck, except they did not use the word aleck. Trudy seemed to welcome his lighthearted conversation and humorous dialogue. If he talked about his business, his wives would complain that he was being impolite or that he was being a bore. Trudy seemed interested in his work, and she shared equal details about her growing business.

There was something more about this woman that attracted him. Freddie could not put his finger on it. As their conversation continued, his subconscious mind replayed the way Trudy smacked him on the back. There was something familiar about it. She dropped her right arm back behind her. She turned slightly on her feet. Her left arm came slightly in front of her body. She hit his back right in the sweet spot and then she followed through. That was it! The perfect tennis forehand! Freddie exclaimed, "Trudy, are you a tennis player?"

Trudy said with pride, "Yes, I love to play. I played in high school and even went to states. Do you play, Freddie?"

"Yes, there is not much I love to do more than play tennis. We should play a game this weekend."

"I would love that!" Trudy said, with a little too much enthusiasm in her voice, she told herself later.

The welcome reception was going well and the Friday family ratings among the groom's family were moving up the scale. Lady was nodding and listening to Auden's dad talk in depth about a car race or a football game, she was not really sure which. It involved something about a finish line or a goal line and something about hitting the fence or was it hitting the defense.

A woman dressed in a black tunic with a white collar around her neck wandered into the room. She had dark brown hair pulled back rather tightly into a small bun and brown glasses resting just below the bridge of her nose. Lady had been looking for a way out of the conversation with Auden's dad, and so excused herself to welcome the newcomer. Her first thought was that they would be witnessing another pantomime, but once she got closer, she noticed that this woman was a member of the clergy, not a mime.

"Welcome," said Lady holding out her hand. "Are you here for the wedding rehearsal? You must be the ministrix. I am the bride's aunt, Lady Friday."

The newcomer spoke with great affectation. "Yes. I am Ministrix Beatrix. I will be conducting the rehearsal tonight and officiating the wedding tomorrow. I am quite delighted to preside over this happy gathering."

"We are very glad to have you and I know my sister thinks you are a miracle sent from the universe," Lady said.

The ministrix blushed demurely. "I am but a servant sent to guide two souls safely across the sea to the shores of eternal love. Your kind words are like rain on a thirsty flower."

As Lady offered her a glass of wine, the ministrix said, "To me marriage is like a rich wine made from two grapes from different vines, don't you think?" She gladly accepted a glass of wine and a loaded her plate with appetizers.

Lady had never thought of marriage as a rich wine

or people as grapes, so she changed the subject. "Beatrix, what a beautiful name. Do people call you Bea?"

"Thank you. My mother named me after the woman in Dante's Paradisio," she said, exaggerating the name Dante to sound like Dan-tay. She added, "And people do not call me Bea. I prefer Beatrix."

Lady said in an excited tone, "How interesting. Do you read Dante? I am working my way through Dorothy Sayers's translation."

Beatrix became unsettled. Her eyes widened as she took a bite of salmon rillettes. She did not think anyone would know anything about Dante, much less the names of translators. She thought to herself, "What happened to the uneducated masses?" Thinking quickly, she said, "Sayers's translation? Uh, er that is a good one. I think you should keep reading Dante and never ever give up." She was relieved when Deidre, Frances, and Ella interrupted the conversation.

"Welcome, Ministrix," said Deidre, grabbing her hands and bending her head over in a sort of bowing motion. "Thank you so much for coming and filling in at the last minute."

Lady, noticing her sister's awkward groveling to this person, could not contain her words. "Deidre. This woman is not the Pope or the Queen of England. You don't have to bow before her or kiss her ring or anything."

Deidre defended herself. "I'm showing respect for a spiritual person, Lady."

The ministrix was humbled at this show of adoration, yet she agreed with Lady. "Your sister is right. I am just a fellow spirit in the great oneness of spirits and so no better than anyone else. Ask not what I can do for you but, er, uh … what we can all do for each other."

This odd spiritual leader intrigued Frances. She decided to probe further and asked, "What religion or church are you affiliated with?"

"None at all," said the ministrix emphatically. "I do not bind myself to any one particular belief system. I am open to them all and so I can perform my spiritual duties for all people. I have malice toward none and charity for all. We are all like the strings of a violin that quiver together making beautiful music and the only thing we have to fear is uh er … fear itself."

The ministrix turned to Ella and examined her jewelry intently. "Those pearls suit you, my dear. You are like a beautiful cedar growing in the shade of an oak adorned with the fruit of the sea. But what is outward adornment but a reflection of the beauty within ourselves?"

Ella was not sure what the ministrix meant but was flattered and said, "These are my grandmother's pearls. They are priceless. I am also wearing them tomorrow for the wedding."

The ministrix said, "But surely, you can't dance with all those pearls weighing you down. Don't you want to be free to dance without any material encumbrances holding you back? This is your finest hour."

Ella answered, "Oh, I have thought of that. I'm going to take off this necklace and put on a different one for the reception. It has just as many pearls but it's shorter. I don't know why but I love wearing jewelry."

The ministrix smiled in agreement with the lovely young bride. "Some people see jewelry and ask why? I see beautiful jewelry and ask why not? You are very sensible to change necklaces and protect your grandmother's heirloom jewelry. Sounds like you have thought of everything."

Thomas and Alexandra walked up and were introduced to the ministrix. Thomas asked, "Have we met before, Ministrix? Your face seems very familiar."

Beatrix answered quickly, "No, no. I am sure we have never met but I am a friend to all people in need. I am a friend indeed."

The ministrix took Alexandra's hand and said, "Your necklace is lovely, my dear. There must be over thirty diamonds and they look like fine quality. The Friday family is blessed with bounteous treasures from the earth. Diamonds are like the tears that the moon gives us on a dark night, don't you think?"

Everyone was processing the diamond analogy with perplexed expressions on their faces. Finally Frances said, "Ministrix, you seem to know a lot about jewelry. Is it a hobby of yours?"

The ministrix eyed Frances closely and answered, "No, no I am just a humble admirer of the manifold treasures that Mother Earth has scattered like seeds across the planet. Speaking of treasures, these appetizers are very good. I wouldn't mind a refill."

Deidre led the ministrix away to refill her plate. Thomas leaned over to Lady and Frances and said in a voice that was not a whisper, "I don't understand anything she is saying. What does she mean? It all sounds like a string of nonsense."

Frances answered, "None of us really understand her either but Deidre really likes her so that's all that matters. Also, the ministrix was willing to come at the last minute and evidently is qualified to officiate a wedding so we should be happy."

The wedding rehearsal at the Flagler Museum was not well organized and did not, in Frances's opinion, go very well. She noticed that the ministrix was over-whelmed with the large wedding party. Her singsong voice was replaced by irritated shouts as she lost control of the group. To Frances, it looked as if the ministrix had never been to a wedding, much less officiated one. The ministrix contradicted herself constantly and her speech was so odd, like a cross between a political speechwriter and a new age guru. Frances had an uneasy feeling about the ministrix. There was was something that bothered her, but she could not put her finger on it.

– Thirteen –
Road Trip

IN A SMALL COLLEGE TOWN IN NORTH CAROLINA there is a popular coffee shop called the Cuppola. The proprietors had always dreamed of opening a coffee shop upon retirement. They leased a storefront, which had a unique architectural element on the roof directly above the front door known as a cupola. The husband, being a man who liked puns and was fond of wordplays, wanted to name the coffee shop "The Cuppola." He envisioned his clientele reaching for the front door handle, looking at the sign over the entrance reading "Cuppola" and noticing the cupola on the roof and thinking, "There must be a clever, witty genius behind this enterprise."

His wife consented to this name, as it was better than the many other names he came up with. When they were considering an extended dinner menu, he had put forth the "Cuppa & Suppa." When they thought about adding a spiritual bookstore, he suggested the "Cuppa Room." And when he wanted to serve a local bakery's gourmet pies and attract a tonier crowd, he thought the name should be "Cuppercrust."

In reality, no one ever noticed the play on words

between "Cuppola" and the cupola on the building. Still, the name was easy to remember and they served good coffee, so it was a popular spot. The Cuppola carried the architectural theme of the exterior into the interior of the café with dark rustic hardwood floors, white painted brick, and large farmhouse style tables for the patrons to enjoy their coffee, study, and socialize.

On a Thursday night, around one of the farmhouse tables, sat undergrads Harley, Chad, and Graham. For the past three years, they had formed a kind of rat pack that followed Auden Woods around Hanlon College. Upon graduation Auden returned to Florida. One of life's hard truths is that life changes and things do not go on as they were. The undergrads were having a hard time starting their senior year of college without their leader. Chad looked up from his books, unable to concentrate, and said, "I really miss Auddie. It is not the same this year."

"Yeah, me too," said Harley. "I hope he is having fun in Florida."

Within days of his arrival at Hanlon in his freshman year, Auden Woods became affectionately known as Auddie on campus. A sharper group of undergrads would have capitalized on the last name "Woods" and come up with the nickname "Woody." Instead they chose to modify his first name and he was dubbed Auddie, the name the inner circle called him from that time onward.

These privileged undergrads, as well as practically everyone else on campus, thought Auden Woods was the coolest guy on the planet; they wanted to be just like him. They dressed like him, they talked like him, they ordered their coffee like him, and they followed him on social media. Chad and Harley were trying to grow a moustache just like him. Auddie did not really say anything brilliant or witty, nor did he ever do anything really daring or successful. He achieved a sort of permanent coolness by getting over 1,500 followers on Instagram. Auddie did not have to do anything. He just had to hang out, be himself, and post to social media on a regular basis, and that was enough.

This popularity, although some may say was unearned, is the main factor that made him appealing to Ella Birnam. Before she started college she had determined what kind of guy she would date. She left behind the uninteresting high school boys and determined to date only guys with over 900 followers on social media. She knew she would probably meet and marry a guy in college, so she was going to set the standard high at the beginning of her freshman year and stick to it.

"Of course he's having fun," interjected Graham. "He's getting married in two days to the hottest Hanlon graduate."

"I wish we could be there," said Harley. "Remember the spring break trip we took to Fort Lauderdale. Auddie rented a van and we drove all night and stayed at that cheap hotel on the beach." They all laughed and sighed as they remembered the trip. Good times.

Something like an illuminated light bulb could be seen over Chad's head as he said, "Why don't we do it again?"

"What, drive to Florida? Now? And do what?" said Graham.

"Go to Florida for Auddie's wedding," explained Chad.

"But we weren't invited," Graham pointed out.

Chad said, "So? Ella's family can afford it. I'm sure they'll have plenty of food."

Harley added, "I sure would like to see the wedding. I bet it's going to be awesome."

Another Hanlon undergrad, Chrissy, overheard their conversation while she was waiting for her coffee. She was a tall girl with blue eyes and curly blond hair. This evening, she wore that "I've been studying in the library too long" look. Her clothes were mismatched, her eyes looked tired, and the curls on her right side were smashed against her head. She was wearing her thick glasses because her eyes were too irritated to wear her contacts. No one stared at her because this was a typical look for Chrissy. Although attractive, she did not spend a lot of time on her appearance. She was more motivated by making good grades than trying to look good all the time. In her opinion, she did not have the time to bother with clothes, hair, and makeup.

She picked up her coffee and took a seat at the table. "I actually got an invitation to Auden and Ella's wedding," she said. "I didn't reply because of classes and exams. Who plans a wedding in October? It's almost as if they did not want us to come."

Chad said in an excited voice, "Perfect! You were invited so you have to go with us."

"What? That is crazy. We can't just drive to Florida for the weekend. I have two tests next week and I'm not sure how I did on my exam today," she said, trying sound like a model student.

"You'll be fine," said Chad dismissively. "You already have like a 3.9999 GPA. Why can't you take one weekend off? You can study on the ride down."

An impromptu trip to South Florida did sound appealing, even to a rational thinker like Chrissy. Her brain could do with a rest, and she had read research that said that a vacation actually made you more productive. She pictured herself in a swimsuit on a warm sunny beach—not freezing in an oversized sweatshirt like the one she was wearing. She asked, "Do you think they'll mind if we show up last minute? Should I text them and RSVP?"

"Of course not! Auddie will be glad to see us and the RSVP thing is no big deal. The old people get hung up on that sort of thing but nobody our age does," said Chad, trying to sound like a wedding etiquette expert.

Harley interjected, "I don't think we should tell Auddie or Ella. I think we should surprise them. They'll be so happy that we took the time to drive down and see them. I can just see the look on their faces."

"Where will we stay and how will we get there?" asked Graham.

Chad, being the enthusiast in the group, was already on the computer looking for rooms to rent in the area. He spun his laptop around and said, "Here is a condo right on the beach that says it sleeps five. It would be affordable if we all split the cost."

Harley added, "I can probably borrow a van from my brother's used car lot. That way we can take one car and split the cost of gas."

Chad said, "This is perfect. I am so psyched. This trip will be epic."

Harley repeated, "I can't wait to see the look on their faces. Graham, Chrissy, are you in?"

Chrissy raised her coffee cup and said with enthusiasm, "I'm in!"

Graham hesitated, "I don't know. I have two tests next week."

Chad explained, "We can take turns driving and you can study in the van. Come on, Graham, don't be a party pooper."

Not wanting to be lame and not wanting to miss an epic trip, Graham finally said, "I guess I'm in."

The undergrads spent the rest of the evening getting ready for the trip. Chrissy ran to several adjoining dorm rooms to borrow a swimsuit, dress, and shoes. Harley called his brother and secured a van, but more importantly he fed his goldfish and gave instructions on their care to his roommate. Chad and Graham stuffed flip-flops, board shorts, and their best dress clothes into duffle bags.

Very early Friday morning, Harley pulled up to the circular drive in front of the Hanlon dorms in the borrowed van. It is a good thing that the loaner was a fifteen-passenger van, because by the time the news had spread about a trip to Florida, the number of undergrads attending the wedding had grown to thirteen.

Graham rubbed his eyes and said, "What is this? Are we going to Palm Beach in a church van?"

The words that almost did not fit on the side of the white van read "First United Separatists Free Congregational Church of the Redeemed Brethren." In addition there were several bumper sticker variations of the ichthys, the fish-shaped Christian symbol, on the bumper. Rounding out the church van look was the "Honk if you love Jesus" sticker on the back window.

"Yes! Do you have a problem with it?" said Harley, grumpy from lack of sleep. "This is all my brother had on the lot on such short notice. It's big enough to hold all of us and he's letting us use it for fifty bucks."

Before the majority of students at Hanlon woke up Friday morning, the thirteen undergrads, or as Auddie sometimes called them, "fun-dergrads," were packed into the van headed to sunny Florida. This brilliant idea concocted within the span of only ten minutes by students in a coffee shop did have some inherent problems and potential pitfalls, but what is the fun in pointing those out? Only a killjoy would think about the bad etiquette of showing up to an elegant wedding uninvited. Only a person sucking the fun out of a situation would wonder how to fit thirteen people into a vacation rental that advertised a five-person max capacity. Only a stick-in-the-mud would worry about what Ella's mother would do to these scoundrels who crashed her daughter's perfect wedding. Those were thoughts going through Graham's mind, but he did not want to sound like a fuddy-duddy, so he buried them in his brain and put his pillow against the window of the van and fell asleep.

It is not surprising that the plan for all the non-drivers to diligently study did not work quite like envisioned. Harley drove and the others slept. After three hours on the road, they took a short pit stop. As they piled back into the van, Chrissy sat in the front because she was getting motion sick in the back of the van. After their short nap and a coffee, the undergrads were fully awake. Their lively conversation as they traveled through South Carolina gravitated to the topic of personality traits and what faction they would each be put into from the movie *Divergent*.

"I would definitely be in the Dauntless faction," said Chad with confidence.

"Do you even know what 'dauntless' means, Chad?" asked Graham.

Chad quickly looked it up on his phone and answered, "Yes, I know what it means. It means brave or fearless. That's totally me. What are you, Graham? Candor?"

Harley looked in the rearview mirror. "I would be in Dauntless too."

They all laughed, including Chrissy, which surprised and stung Harley more than he expected.

"Harley, you are the least dauntless person I know," said Chad. "You have goldfish and a turtle in your dorm room."

Graham, knowing the meaning of the factions, said, "Harley, you fit more into Amity or Abnegation."

Harley protested, "But I want to be dauntless. A person can determine what they want to be. I don't have to be what you say I am."

"You can't pick your faction," said Graham. "It is your natural personality—the way you were born. A tiger can't change his spots."

"That's stupid," said Harley who really wanted to be seen by his peers as dauntless. "A tiger does not have spots. It is just a silly movie anyway."

"Graham is right," said Chrissy. She was well-read on personality types and was always interested in trying to understand how people thought. She added, "I think a person is born with certain traits. There are things they are really good at and some areas where they have weaknesses. We should be happy with who we are. We are not all supposed to be the same."

She could tell Harley was not happy about being categorized. She did not want him to feel bad about himself, so she added, "Abnegation is a great trait in a man, Harley. You stayed up all night getting the van for us. You are driving so everyone else can sleep. You have not asked anyone for gas money. You are acting selfless. Great leaders are selfless."

Harley was not used to this kind of probing into his personality, especially by an intelligent girl, and it made him uncomfortable. He had never thought much about his personality. He was just Harley, and he seemed to get along with everyone just fine. As he thought more about it, he was touched by her comments and gave her a smile to show his appreciation. He asked her, "Which faction are you?"

She answered quickly, "I am Erudite."

"I can see that," said Harley. "But you are a nice Erudite," he added.

She smiled back and for a few awkward seconds it seemed like they were having a romantic moment. Harley's heart started beating faster. He was not sure what was happening to him. He wanted to keep the conversation going but didn't know what to say. Finally he blurted out, "Seen any good movies lately?" As soon as the words came out of his mouth he looked out the driver's side window and told himself, "That was a stupid question. Dumb, dumb, dumb. You can do better. What would Auden do?"

Chrissy thought for a minute and then answered, "I like old movies. So when I have free time, I watch some of the classics. You know, Humphrey Bogart or Cary Grant."

Harley said, "I think I watched a Cary Grant movie with my sister once. It was the one where he is being chased by an airplane. I liked Cary Grant in that movie. He was so smooth."

Chrissy named the movie. "*North by Northwest*. That is a classic. I love all Cary Grant movies, especially that one!"

Harley nodded and said, "Me too." He was not really sure what made a movie a classic. He also made a mental note to watch more Cary Grant movies.

The conversations in the van died down as one by one the undergrads opened their books to study. Within five minutes, they were all asleep like babies who are strapped into their car seats. Harley was still in the driver's seat when they crossed over the Florida state line. He started to make an announcement but as he looked in the rearview mirror, he saw all the passengers piled on top of each other still fast asleep. Luckily, the road noise and the mellow music on the playlist drowned out the sound of random car horns honking as they noticed the stickers on the van. Harley thought to himself, "There sure are a lot of Jesus lovers in Florida."

Harley's excitement grew as he read the billboards along Interstate 95. The colorful advertisements were trying to draw visitors to the Kennedy Space Center, the original Ron Jon's surf shop in Cocoa Beach, to Disney World in Orlando or to the many golf courses along the coast. Harley knew his final destination did not include any of these places, but he was thrilled to be driving into one of the most visited places on earth. This impromptu adventure, combined with the warm sunshine, caused a feeling of empowerment to come over him. He was ready to take some risks. He thought, "I will show them who is dauntless."

– Fourteen –
The Boca Break In

IT DID NOT TAKE MUCH to make Freddie Friday happy. Good food, good company, and the thought of breaking into his ex-wife's house had put him in a sunny mood. He was smiling, relaxed, and feeling goodwill towards all people as the newly formed burglary gang headed south on A1A. He liked this company of women in the car. No one was badgering him or criticizing him or trying to make him feel like he was a dumb oaf. Lady was often curt and direct, but he knew she was a devoted sister. And he always liked being with Frances. He started to reminisce about other times in the past Frances had pitched in to help solve a family problem. He said, "Alexandra, this is not the first time your Aunt Frances has helped us out of a jam."

Speaking to the driver, he said, "Franny, remember the birthday debacle with Tiffany?"

"Of course I remember," said Frances, smiling at Freddie in the rearview mirror.

"What happened? Who is Tiffany again?" said Alexandra.

Freddie said, "Tiffany was my second wife. She was a beautiful girl with golden blonde hair, blue eyes, white teeth—the whole package. She was very into fitness and healthy eating. Most men gain a few pounds the first year of marriage. I lost fifteen pounds our first year of marriage."

"You certainly have a type, Freddie," said Lady, shaking her head.

"I suppose I do have a type. Anyway, Tiffany came to our marriage with a one-year-old baby. I didn't realize it at the time, but she was very self-conscious about the weight she had gained during her pregnancy. I thought she looked great, but she was unhappy with her body. Her birthday was coming up and I had a perfect gift idea. What do you give a person into fitness? You give them fitness-related items, right?"

"So, I took her out to a nice dinner and had a four-tiered gift, beautifully wrapped, sitting on the table. After dinner she was so excited to open her gift. The first layer was a very expensive set of designer workout clothes. She did not have the excited look I was anticipating on her face. The second box contained the most expensive running shoes I could find. Again her face seemed perplexed rather than joyful. The third layer had a membership to an exclusive gym and the fourth box that looked like a jewelry box did not contain jewelry but a Fitbit. By the time she opened the fourth box, she was in tears and ran out of the restaurant sobbing. She Ubered home and locked herself in the bathroom after the babysitter left. She would not come out and talk to me. She said she was on a hunger strike.

"I tell you, I was not prepared for this kind of drama. I was living near Frances and Sam at the time, so I put out the distress call. Frances came to our house in the middle of the night and talked to Tiffany. She got her out of the bathroom and into my arms in thirty minutes flat. I tell you this woman is a miracle worker. Although, I think you purposely included a harsh punishment for me in your solution."

"Fitness wear and a gym membership for your new wife's birthday," scoffed Lady. "What were you thinking? Deidre and I trained you better than that."

"You most certainly did not!" protested Freddie. "You should have provided more drama in my childhood. I mean, what are sisters for but to prepare a man to deal with situations like that? I could have used some more emotional instability from you. You let me down. Even though Deidre got upset and threw things at me, she never locked herself in rooms or went on hunger strikes. I was like a tiny boat in a hurricane during my marriage to Tiffany."

"What did you say, Aunt Frances?" asked Alexandra. "What did you say to make Tiffany feel better?"

"After talking it over with Freddie, I told Tiffany that he had not given her the final part of the gift. He had planned an anniversary trip to France without kids. The clothes and the gym membership were to prepare for the strenuous Tour de Mont Blanc trail. I told her he wanted to train with her for the next six months so that they could spend time together and prepare for a romantic anniversary trip."

Freddie said, "Tiffany loved the idea because there is nothing like a fitness freak with a challenging goal. The training and the hundred-mile hike almost killed me, but it made her very happy—for a while anyway. It was pure genius; you never know what Frances will come up with. She is like the Friday family angel. Without Frances, our family would be like Bedford Falls without George Bailey."

Alexandra was puzzled. "Who is George Bailey and where is Bedford Falls?"

"Oh, you know that guy from the movie *It's a Wonderful Life*. The angel shows him what life would be like if he was not there. The whole town would be in a shambles because he was never born. We watch the movie every Christmas. It is a Friday family tradition. You have never seen it? I can't believe Thomas never watched it with you. That borders on child abuse. Well, we will have to watch it together this Christmas."

"I am hardly an angel, but I appreciate the compliment," said Frances. She had always felt a little awkward about getting involved in Freddie's marriage problems. She was so fond of Freddie, but where should she draw the line? Was she enabling people by jumping in and helping them just because she was capable? Was she really an angel if she stretched the truth to get them out of bad situations? And now, tonight, it was her idea to break into a house to solve the latest problem. She told herself that it was better to be helpful than to let them flounder. She would think more about it later because they had arrived. She pulled the car into the cul-de-sac at the end of the neighborhood and turned off her headlights.

She whispered, "Okay, Freddie. We will wait here. You go ahead."

"What! You are not going to send me on this mission alone!" he protested. "I need a partner, a sidekick, someone to keep lookout and lend a hand if this goes sideways."

Alexandra volunteered and insisted she was the best accomplice. "All dogs love me," she explained.

Freddie and Alexandra walked past the tall green hedges that surrounded the beautiful homes. A couple Freddie did not recognize walked toward them on the opposite side of the street. Freddie and Alexandra stalled, acting nonchalant, as nonchalant as two people can act in a beach community at night wearing all black and having their pockets stuffed with stew meat. Luckily, the couple passed by without noticing them.

Crossing the lawn, Freddie popped the latch on the side gate and led Alexandra past the pool equipment and air conditioners. He punched in the code on the keypad to open the side door and turned off the alarm system. Lance had told Freddie that his mother never changed the default security codes. Freddie thought, "What good is a security system when you never change the codes?" This was another point of contention in their marriage, but tonight his ex-wife's haphazard security measures worked to his advantage.

He eased the door open and threw a scrap of meat in the middle of the laundry room floor in case the Pekes were alerted to their presence. Alexandra thought this level of caution was a little exaggerated for a few small dogs. She could understand if they were guard dogs, but this was a little absurd.

Freddie whispered for Alexandra to stay in the laundry room and keep a lookout. He did not hear any barking or growling so he tiptoed into the house using his phone light to light the way. He made his way to the master bedroom on the opposite side of the house and expected to find the automatic winding case that had held his watches in the closet. Neither the case nor the watches were there. He searched the bedroom, the bathroom, and the spare bedroom but could not find the watches. He regrouped with Alexandra and whispered to her, "I can't find the watches. I can't find any of my old things. I'm going to try Susan's office, although I don't know why my things would be in there."

Freddie's ex-wife heartily believed the saying that "a wagging tail and a friendly woof brings joy to all beneath the roof." Susan wanted to pack as much joy within the three thousand square feet of her beach house as possible. This fact and the melancholy feeling following her divorce had caused the dog count under her roof to more than double.

On the other side of the office door a very courageous little dog that looked like a shaggy mop with a black face was standing like a general ready to give the battle cry. Susan's prizewinning Pekingese dog, Trixie-Boo, had tried to take her morning nap, earlier in the day, on the divan in the master bedroom. She could not sleep because her owner insisted on going in and out of the closet, packing an overnight bag. She knew her owner was going out of town and as per usual, the boy, Lance, would come to walk and feed her and the other dogs.

Tonight, her keen ears detected that there were multiple humans padding around her house. And they did not smell like Lance. She caught the scent of a human she particularly disliked. Trixie-Boo was exhilarated. This would be no ordinary night, and she could almost taste the adventure in the air. She lived up to the name the Chinese had given to the Pekingese breed, "lion dog." She had the heart of a lion and was the undisputed leader of the motley assortment of dogs in the house. With her ears perked up and her heart racing, she was ready to lead them in defending their home.

Freddie was not aware of the canine army assembled on the other side of the door. He put his hand to the handle, cracked the door, and immediately heard a cacophony of growls and barks. He was startled at first but then began to be afraid as a very large dog with very big teeth and a very threatening growl pushed the door open and lunged toward him. Freddie bolted toward the kitchen and jumped up on the counter, banging his head on the copper pots that hung from the French pot rack over the large kitchen island.

This pot rack was another point of contention in their marriage. Being a tall man, he did not understand why they paid thousands of dollars to renovate the kitchen with solid wood cabinets and then hang all the pots from the ceiling. He had often hit his head on them as he did now. He was glad, however, that they had agreed to make the kitchen island another two feet wider, as he was able to sit in the center away from the reach of the ferocious dog. Hearing the barking and seeing the parade of dogs chasing Freddie, Alexandra adroitly jumped on top of the washing machine. They looked at each other and realized that whispering was no longer necessary.

Freddie shouted as he was slinging meat toward the assembled dogs, "Great! Susan has rescued more dogs, including a German shepherd."

The fierce sounding shepherd did not let up its baritone bark and was growling and baring its teeth. Luckily Susan had a soft spot for older dogs and its aging hips did not allow it to jump up on the counter to devour Freddie.

"Uncle Freddie, how are we going to get out of the house?" asked Alexandra.

Hearing Alexandra's voice for the first time, the Pekes, led by Trixie-Boo, ran to the laundry room and started barking at her. She did not realize how shrill and loud small dogs could be. She was reconsidering her earlier statement that all dogs loved her. She said in a soothing voice, "Good doggies. Who wants some meat?" The Pekes would not be quieted. She distributed most of the meat in her pockets and gave her uncle a "what now?" look.

Freddie shouted, "Call Frances. I left my phone in the car. Tell her to come to the side door and bring more meat."

Alexandra called the other gang members, explaining the addition of a German shepherd and how they were trapped. Moving her phone away from her face and placing her hand over it, she yelled to Freddie, "Aunt Frances wants to know how far it is from the kitchen to the front door."

"What? How far? I don't know, about sixty feet give or take a few feet? Why?"

Getting more information, Alexandra yelled to him the plan, "Aunt Frances is going to go to the front door and bang on the door and ring the doorbell. She thinks the dogs will run to the front door and bark at her, leaving us time to get out the side door. Aunt Lady will come to the side door with more meat just in case."

"Okay, tell them to hurry. I'm sure the neighbors can hear this infernal noise."

As he waited for the doorbell signal, Freddie emptied the remaining bloody meat from his pocket onto the counter. At the sound of the front doorbell chime, Trixie-Boo led the barking pack to the front door to dutifully guard the front. Freddie jumped off the island, bolted through the laundry room behind Alexandra and out the door that Lady was holding open.

"What do I do with the rest of this meat?" Lady said, holding it far away from her person.

"Leave it! Close the door!" said Freddie, sprinting past her.

She flung the extra meat into the laundry room and slammed the door. The dogs regrouped at the side door and were temporarily quiet while they consumed the meat scraps.

Absent from the pack was their fearless leader, Trixie-Boo. She had anticipated the criminals' next move and, using stealth, followed them out the side door. In all the excitement, she felt the need to empty her bladder and so she quickly and quietly ducked into the thick, green hedge to answer nature's call.

Frances walked around the side of the house to see if the mission was a success. Freddie informed her that he could not find the watches. While they stood there trying to rethink the plan, they heard Trixie-Boo emerge from the hedge and start sounding the alarm once more. The other dogs heard their leader and, fearing she was in danger, began to bark in chorus once more at the side door.

While they were looking incredulously at Susan's prizewinning dog barking up at them, Alexandra whispered, "Look! Someone is coming with a flashlight."

When in a stressful situation, people have a choice to flee the scene or to stand and fight. This is commonly known as the fight-or-flight response. Lady and Alexandra's response was to flee, so they simultaneously jumped into the thick green hedge to hide. This left the stronger members of the family, Frances and Freddie, to stand and fight. Acting out of pure adrenal reflex, Freddie scooped up Trixie-Boo and stuffed her into the backpack he had brought to stash the watches and any other items he retrieved from the beach house.

The neighbor lifted the gate latch and walked towards them, shining a light in their faces. He said what any good neighbor under these odd circumstances would say, "What is going on here? Did you just put a Pekingese in your backpack?"

Although Trixie-Boo was still barking loudly from the confines of the backpack, Freddie's knee jerk response was, "Pekingese? What? No!"

Frances was a quick thinker. Within seconds, her mind scanned several possible scenarios that would satisfy this neighbor and prevent him from calling the police. If she had more time she would have come up with something better. The plan she settled on was not ideal. In fact it was the most absurd, but she proceeded anyway, hoping it would turn out well.

"Goot eefning! I am assisting ziss man with a very delicate treatment for his dog. Yah! As you say, we do have a doggie in zee backpack. It is part of zee treatment. But do not alarm yourself. It is goot for her. Yah."

Freddie looked with surprise and admiration at Frances. He quickly joined in on the improvisational story. "Oh, yes, let me introduce you to Dr. Freudenschnauzer, the eminent dog nerve specialist. I am sure you have heard of her. She is the best in the world."

The neighbor looked unconvinced, so Frances continued, "It is important zat we continue with zee treatment. Ziss doggie has to undergo a sensory deprivation experience of total isolation; zat is why we put her in zee black backpack at night. You have interrupted our important work at zee critical stage. We need to continue with zee delicate process, so we bid you goot night."

The neighbor recognized Freddie and said, "I thought you and Susan split up, so why are you here giving her dog treatments?"

Freddie was stumped and looked to the good doctor to give the man an answer. Frances continued, "Ziss is all part of the doggie's problem. She has trouble breaking through to zee higher levels of dog show competitions and we have narrowed zee problem down to Freddie."

Freddie caught the drift and joined in. "Yes, Trixie-Boo still holds resentment towards me and only I can help her overcome her abandonment issues since the divorce. She needs to be able to forgive me and move on. Pekingese hold grudges worse than ex-wives."

"Ah, Ah," interrupted Frances. "Frederick! Remember what I said about negative statements like zat. Zey only make our job harder."

"I am sorry, doctor, you are right," Freddie reassured her. Turning to the neighbor he said, "Now, what was your name, Bill? You can see that everything is perfectly normal here so please let us continue with our work without any more interruptions."

Just then, Alexandra's nose demanded relief, and so a loud sneeze was heard coming out of the hedge. The neighbor shone the flashlight toward the direction of the sneeze and Lady and Alexandra stepped out of the thick hedge, not aware that small twigs were sticking out of their hair.

Lady, having overheard the conversation with the neighbor, joined in on the charade. "Doctor Freudenschnauzer, I do not think the hedges covered our scent. The Pekingese is still aware of our presence. We are running out of time, don't you think we should start the therapy walk soon?"

"Excellent idea!" said the doctor. "Frederick, you have to wear Trixie-Boo in the backpack while you jog around the neighborhood. I think some skipping unt jumping will also do zee trick. Only in ziss way will you regain her trust once more. She will emerge from zee backpack at a higher level of emotional wellness. We must begin."

As the bewildered neighbor watched them walk away, Freddie began skipping and jumping down the sidewalk holding on to the backpack straps. Once they were out of sight, they ran to the car and jumped in. Frances looked at Freddie in the backseat of the car and said, "Freudenschnauzer? Could that name sound more fake?"

Freddie defended himself. "Well, I'm usually good at improvisation but this time I choked. That name just popped into my head."

Freddie let Trixie-Boo out of the backpack. She was so grateful on being freed from her dark prison that she decided not to bite him.

Frances said, "We'll wait twenty minutes for the neighbor to go back home and then sneak Trixie-Boo back into the house."

"Hold on," said Freddie. "I have an idea. Since I couldn't find the watches, I think I know another way to have Lance call off the protest. If I can't persuade him with money, maybe I can motivate him with fear."

"We are all ears," said Lady.

As he petted Trixie-Boo's head, he said with a smile, "We have something more valuable than watches. Susan left Lance in charge of her prizewinning Peke. If she found out Lance allowed her dog to be taken, she would pitch a huge fit and probably cut him off and kick him out. I will contact Lance and tell him if he ever wants to see Trixie-Boo again, he has to call off the protest immediately."

Freddie handed Trixie-Boo to Alexandra and took out his phone as Frances sped away from the crime scene. Lance was disappointed not to get the money from Freddie, but he still agreed to call off the protest in exchange for the dog's return. Freddie, rather proud of his role in saving the wedding, said, "Mission accomplished! Tomorrow, I will drop the dog off on the way to the wedding."

Lady was in the habit of pointing out the problems in her brother's schemes. She asked, "Why don't we return the dog tonight. Why tomorrow? Are you planning on smuggling a dog into The Breakers?"

Freddie protested. "Smuggling? You make us sound like criminals. No, we can't return her yet. I don't trust Lance to keep his word. We won't know until tomorrow if he called off the rally. We will have to sneak the dog into the hotel. We can't leave her in the car all night. Don't worry. Trust me." They all agreed that, although not a perfect plan, it was their only option.

Alexandra giggled as Trixie-Boo licked her hands incessantly. She and Freddie noticed dried meat blood not only on their hands but also down their wrists. Freddie said, "I feel a little like Lady Macbeth with this blood on my hands."

Frances, being a mother of four, quickly produced a pack of hand-sanitizing wipes and passed it back to the occupants of the back seat. Knowing that his sister could quote Shakespeare at the drop of a hat, Freddie asked, "Lady, what is the line from Macbeth? You know after Lady Macbeth says 'out damned spot'?"

Lady did not disappoint. She said with no hesitation in her best Shakespearian accent, "'Here is the smell of blood still. All the perfumes in Arabia will not sweeten this little hand.'"

Freddie added, "Unlike Lady Macbeth, I do not feel a bit guilty."

– Fifteen –
Early Risers

THE SPECTACULAR FLORIDA SUNRISE on the day of the wedding was missed by the Hanlon undergrads. They slept soundly as a dog barked at a squirrel at six o'clock in the morning. They did not wake up when the trash truck banged the trashcans into the dumpster at six thirty. They did not wake up at seven when Harley rose quietly, unhooked his phone from the charger, requested an Uber ride, and slipped out the front door.

The long drive had given Harley the opportunity for reflective thought. Out of his usual surroundings and cloistered in the van with Chrissy for over ten hours, he had come to a decision. This weekend he was going to exert extra effort to try to impress her and if that went well, he would ask her for out. The first step in his plan was to locate a salon in Palm Beach and get a total make-over. How hard could it be? They did it on television every day. He would walk in, show them a picture on his phone and ask them to do their best to make him look like Cary Grant. He called his sister, a stylist, for advice. She worked her connections and got him in with the famous South Florida stylist named Lee Something or did she say Gee?

Guy Gadbois agreed to see Harley very early Saturday morning. He was a romantic at heart and was touched by this young man's plea for help to impress a girl. Harley entered the chic salon feeling quite out of place. He saw a very elegant, well-coiffed man coming towards him.

"Monsieur Harley. Welcome. I am Guy," said the stylist warmly. He stood for a moment sizing up Harley and thinking he should have scheduled another two hours for this appointment.

"Thank you for opening early for me, Mr. Gadbois," said Harley politely. He was not sure how to pronounce Guy.

"You can call me Guy. It is pronounced like bee but with a 'g.' I had to take you early because I am doing a wedding party later today. Let's get started." He wrapped Harley in a black kimono and sat him down in a chair. "Tell me about this girl, Chrissy, was her name?"

Harley had only known Chrissy for a semester, but he found it easy to describe her. He began, "She is really smart and pretty. She really cares about other people and is easy to talk to. My problem is that I feel so awkward around her. Sometimes I feel like she does not take me seriously. I want to look my best so that I have confidence to ask her out."

"L'amour! Young love!" said Guy in an airy tone. "She is smart, eh," he said contemplating. "How does she express herself to the world? Is she a Facebook or Instagram girl? Show me who she is."

"Well, I guess she is more of an Instagram girl," said Harley, never really having thought about it before. He pulled up her profile on his phone and showed Guy some recent posts.

Taking in the information, Guy concluded, "Ahhh! She is direct and to the point—less artistic, more realistic. And she is an accounting major tres bien, very good. Sounds like a no-nonsense girl. She may not take you seriously because your current look does not reflect the man she suspects is on the inside."

"What do you mean?" asked Harley.

"Look at this unstructured, unruly mustache and beard. Look at your curly hair let loose to fend for itself without any boundaries. Look at your baggy tee shirt and dirty shoes with broken laces. You do not show respect for yourself. Naturellement, neither will she. We need to make a few small changes to show this jeune fille the intelligent, caring, debonair man that is hidden beneath all this," said Guy holding up tangled locks of Harley's auburn hair.

Harley was stung by Guy's unflattering head-to-toe assessment of his current look, although, as he saw himself in the mirror, he had to agree. He said with resolve in his voice, "I want you to make me into someone completely different. I want to look like Cary Grant. Like my Granny says, I don't want it to look like you just put lipstick on a pig."

"Your Granny is very wise," said Guy kindly. "But, no! We are not going to change you into someone completely different. We are going to bring out your inner

Cary Grant. I think there is great potential in you, mon ami!"

As he took Harley to the sink to wash and condition his hair, the other stylists arrived and began preparing for a wedding party that was scheduled to get their hair and nails done that morning. Back at the chair, combing through Harley's hair with some effort, Guy inquired, "Let's talk more about your love life. When is the last time you asked a girl to go out with you?"

Harley had to think for a while to remember the last time he asked a girl out. He said, "I asked a girl to a frat party a year ago and I thought we had a good time. When I asked her out again, she said that she did not have time to date anyone because of her studies. Then I asked her again and she said she did not want to date anyone until she graduated. It is a shame because I really liked her. I understood though—she had priorities. I respect that."

"Harley, mon ami," said Guy with a sympathetic tone. "That sounds like a façon de parle."

"What does that mean?" asked Harley.

Guy explained, "Façon de parle. The girl did not want to hurt your feelings so she told you a polite fiction. We are going to make sure that Chrissy does not have to tell you a polite fiction." The conversation died down as Guy became engrossed in his work.

Harley was relaxing in the comfortable salon chair with a black cape around his neck, his hair laden with shiny foils and a stylist buffing his fingernails. He was enjoying this personal attention and was even joining in on the salon gossip among the stylists when Ella Birnam and her bridesmaids walked through the front door.

Harley was shocked and embarrassed. He thought to himself, "Of all the salons in Palm Beach, she had to walk into mine." He slid a *Vogue* magazine in front of his face, hoping he would not be seen. It was too late; one of Ella's bridesmaids was the kind of girl who noticed every detail and quickly sized up everyone in the room. Harley thought she would be a good CIA agent because she placed him as a Hanlon undergrad in less than five minutes.

"Harley! What are you doing here?" she yelled across the salon. Suddenly, Harley was surrounded by a group of women, some with hands on hips, some with their mouths open wide, and Ella, with a nervous smile on her face.

"Harley," said Ella. "Why are you in a salon in Palm Beach? How did you get here?"

"Hi, Ella," he said sheepishly. "It's kind of a funny story. We all missed Auden, and you, of course, and we thought it would be fun to surprise you and come to your wedding. Surprise!" he added hoping she would be thrilled and overjoyed at their thoughtfulness.

"When you say 'we,' what do you mean?" she asked.

"Me, Graham, Chad, Chrissy, and about nine others drove all night to get here in time for the wedding."

Ella felt faint. There were only a few hours until the wedding and now this. Why were there so many problems with her wedding? More importantly, how was she going to tell her mother about thirteen uninvited guests? It would surely send her into a panic, and she would develop a migraine and probably not recover in time for the ceremony. Not being a quick thinker or an experienced problem solver, she began to despair.

Ella said to the bridesmaids and Harley, "I'll be right back." She darted out of the salon into the open air to catch her breath. The beautiful sunshine and the fresh air, although normally therapeutic, were not able to calm her. Her thoughts were rapid and chaotic. She took another deep breath and tried not to slide into an emotional funk. A bird chirped overhead and the words "Aunt Frances" popped into her mind. As the other bridesmaids asked Harley questions about the spontaneous road trip, Ella called her Aunt Frances.

"Help, Aunt Franny!" Ella exclaimed, "Thirteen of Auden's friends drove all night and are coming to the wedding—uninvited. I'm talking to one at the salon now. Should I tell them they can't come because they were not invited? I don't want to make them mad at me. I am so upset. I don't know what to do."

Frances was silent for a moment, which caused Ella to raise her voice. "Aunt Franny, what should I do?"

Frances knew her niece was excitable on a normal day and this day, being her wedding day, had the potential of sending her into hysterics. She decided she would give Ella a favorable answer to calm her nerves and then she would worry about how to solve the problem later. She answered with an upbeat, positive voice. "Don't ask them to leave. They must be very fond of you and Auden to have come all this way. Let your friends know you are happy they came and that they are very welcome at the wedding. I will talk to your mother and we will figure it out. You don't need to worry about a thing. Enjoy your morning. It will be fine."

Reassured, Ella entered the salon, changed her expression from panic to delight, and said to Harley, "I am so glad you came! What a nice surprise."

The bridesmaid that was a future candidate for the CIA pressed him further. "Harley, why are you in a high end salon with foils in your hair. What is going on?"

Vulnerability had come over Harley since entering this posh salon. He had never felt this way when getting his usual ten-dollar haircut. In this atmosphere he felt he could be himself, that he could share his feelings and emotions freely without fear or judgment. He felt he could tell these women gathered around him the secret he had only just discovered himself in a van bound for Florida. He confessed that he thought Chrissy was the bomb and related his intention to woo her at the wedding. The women were delighted at the story of secret love and wanted to help Harley. They all agreed. "We totally 'ship' you and Chrissy!"

As they were getting their manicures, they continued to offer advice on his wardrobe, things to say and not to say to her. And they gave him all their intel on Chrissy's likes and dislikes. Guy chimed in with his suggestions as he trimmed Harley's bushy eyebrows.

After Harley's transformation was complete, Guy proudly spun him around in the chair to face the rest of the salon. The bride and bridesmaids were speechless, making Harley uneasy. Ella finally said, "Harley, you look amazing! I mean you have always been a great guy, but look at you now!"

"She is right. You have all you need to woo Chrissy right here," Guy added as he patted his heart. "I just polished the outside a little." Whipping off the cape, he declared, "I want you to walk into the wedding tonight with a confident attitude. How do you say—jaunty."

"Jaunty," repeated Harley. "I like that. I am going to be jaunty." Pausing for a second he said, "What does jaunty mean, exactly?"

Guy explained, "It means a cheerful, self-confident manner. You are like Cary Grant. Comprenez-vous?"

Happy that Guy used Cary Grant to round out the definition, Harley said, "Yes! I understand."

Harley left the salon and walked a few doors down to a men's clothing store and carefully purchased the items Guy and the bridesmaids had suggested for his wedding attire. He was hesitant to spend the money but agreed, on this occasion, as Mark Twain would say, "Clothes make the man." It was time for him to go all in and dress for success.

On his Uber ride back to the condo, Harley noticed he had the most confidence that he had experienced in his young life. He was anxious about the big reveal and was a little disappointed when he walked into the condo and no one was inside. All the undergrads except Chrissy were sitting outside by the pool on every available chair or beach towel eating snacks and drinking Mountain Dew. They looked up and stared at the newcomer with their mouths wide open. The quicker ones realized this was their friend Harley.

Graham asked, "What happened to you? We woke up and you were gone. Where did you go this morning?" He stopped before he said something like we were worried because that would be uncool thing for a guy to say.

"I just went to get a haircut," said Harley nonchalantly. Noticing they were still staring at him with questioning looks he added, "Can't a guy get a haircut before a wedding? Do I have to tell you everywhere I go?" These words seemed to satisfy the group, and no one made fun of him or questioned his new look. They closed their eyes and resumed working on their tans.

When no one challenged him or made fun of him he thought, "Why have I waited so long to get a makeover?" Looking around the pool deck he asked, "Where is Chrissy?"

"She got ready early and left," Chad informed him. "Ella invited her to hang out with them before the wedding started. I don't know how she knew Chrissy was in town." Chad and the other undergrads thought women must be connected in some sort of telepathic way or were like a location satellite that could locate their girlfriends at all times.

Harley did not tell them he had seen Ella and her bridesmaids. He did not want them to know he was the one who blew the surprise. He was partly disappointed and partly relieved Chrissy was not at the condo. He was excited to show her his new look, but now she would get the full effect when he walked into the wedding in his new clothes.

Thomas Friday also rose early on the day of the wedding. He was in a fine mood. His trip the previous day to visit Maria and ask her to be his wedding date had not gone exactly as he had originally imagined, but as Shakespeare would say, "All's well that ends well." Maria would accompany him to the wedding and that was all that mattered.

He opened the drapes and stared out of his window at the perfectly manicured lawn bordered by palm trees, tropical hedges, and a colorful annual bed. As he surveyed the grounds, he wondered how to occupy himself until he was scheduled to pick up Maria. He did not feel like reading. He did not feel like eating. He did not feel like doing work. He felt like being outside. A sense of urgency overtook him. He realized that he was going to be at The Breakers for only one more day and he had not yet inspected the vast grounds and cataloged the plants.

He dressed quickly, grabbed his gardening notebook and his phone, and headed out. After downing coffee and a pastry, he meandered throughout the lushly landscaped property. He admired the simple elegance of the plants used in the Mediterranean courtyard. He wondered how they kept the perfectly green lawns in such immaculate condition. He stood in awe of the impressive fountain topping the main drive. He enthusiastically snapped photos at every stop with his phone and jotted notes in his journal.

Thomas lingered on the pool deck. Even there he saw great attention to landscape detail. He was standing behind a large palm tree, leaning forward trying to get the perfect picture of a tropical flower arrangement in a stone planter, when he realized he was being watched.

A woman directly in front of him with very large breasts and a very skimpy bikini was staring at him with a peevish look on her face. She finally said, "What a pervert." She put on her beach cover-up, slid her feet into her sandals, and left. Thomas felt he should explain that he was taking a picture of the beautiful arrangement but decided to not say those words. He was completely innocent, and the woman had completely misunderstood, but he had learned that it was better not to try to explain. The fact remained that he was a fully dressed, middle-aged man taking pictures in the pool area from behind a palm tree. He made a mental note to not put himself in this situation again.

As he put his phone away he noticed more eyes on him. He was attracting unwanted attention from the other sunbathers. He attempted to blend in and look normal. This was not possible. At that moment another fully dressed, middle-aged man who was soaking wet walked up next to him and started talking. It was his brother Freddie.

"Hello, Thomas! I see you are at your hobby again," said Freddie in a loud voice, innocently referring to plant photography, not voyeurism.

This statement and Freddie's appearance caused more hotel guests to stare, making Thomas very uncomfortable. He finally noticed that his brother was wearing all white but that he was wet from head to toe. He had guessed that Freddie had been playing tennis, but why was he wet? "Freddie, why are you soaking wet?"

Freddie looked down at his wet clothes and tennis shoes and said, "Oh, this does look odd doesn't it. I went swimming just now."

Feeling the explanation still lacked some pertinent details, Thomas asked, "You went swimming in your tennis clothes—and shoes?"

"Well it was not intentional. Trudy jumped in and so I jumped in."

Thomas remembered his mother's words: "Just because someone else jumps in the lake does not mean that you have to jump in too." He was surprised at his little brother ignoring their mother's advice and acting like a fraternity boy at this nice resort.

Freddie provided the missing details. "Trudy and I played tennis this morning and she beat me every single game. I owed her a drink so we stopped at the bar near the pool. I turned to give Trudy her drink and all of a sudden she bolted toward the water and jumped in the deep end. She sailed over the water like a Labrador in one of those dock-jumping competitions. I think she cleared over nine feet before she hit the water. It was spectacular! She took to the water because the lifeguard was having trouble rescuing a very large tourist from drowning. The man was thrashing and fighting and was holding the lifeguard underwater. Trudy grabbed him in a powerful neck hold and calmed him down. It was quite remarkable. What a woman!"

"If Trudy saved him, how did you get wet?" asked Thomas.

"The man passed out from panic, so I jumped in to help get his rather large body out of the pool. I am still pumping with adrenaline. It feels great to take part in a heroic rescue. I can't think of a better way to start the day."

Thomas felt that his morning plant cataloging had come to an end, so he accompanied his soggy brother back into the hotel to get ready for the wedding. He put his hand on his younger brother's sopping back and said, "I am proud of you, Freddie."

– Sixteen –
Wedding Setup

THE EARLY MORNING FLORIDA SUN beamed on the massive white marble columns and the red tile roof of the Flagler Museum. The opulent Beaux Arts style mansion was built during what Mark Twain dubbed the Gilded Age. It was for this reason that Deidre chose it as the perfect venue for her daughter's wedding. Along with the magnificent architecture, she loved the nostalgic, romantic story that Henry Flagler built it as a wedding present for his wife. She became a high-level patron of museum so that she could enjoy the exclusive benefit of holding an event there. The ceremony would take place in the Pavilion, which was modeled after a turn of the century railway palace. The cocktail reception would take place on the lawn overlooking the intracoastal waterway. The dinner and dancing would take place in the West Room.

As wedding vendors arrived at the museum to set up for the big event, they walked past two confused but dedicated protesters straddling their bikes in front of the large iron fence that surrounded the museum. They wore bike shorts, Christmas sweaters, and fake Santa beards. The taller one held a sign that read, "Give trees a chance" and the shorter one's sign read, "Don't be naughty, buy artificial."

Dylan the deejay was the first to arrive. As he walked past the protesters and read their signs, he smiled a good morning smile and said, "Looks like we have a revolution. All right. Don't stop believing."

Lisa Moreno was next to arrive with her two assistants to begin wedding preparations. They passed the two protesters who, by this time, had dismounted their bikes, moved off the bike path, and were standing rather unassumingly in the grass tilting their signs back and forth. Lisa read their signs and thought to herself, "How sad. No one told them that the protest was cancelled." She offered an explanation as she greeted them. "Good morning. I understand that the protest, bicycle rally or whatever, has been called off today so you might as well go home."

The protesters looked at each other and the taller one said to the shorter one, "Check your phone. See if Lance sent a message."

The shorter protester said, "But we agreed to be on a technology fast for a week. You check your phone."

"Well all right," said the taller one, aggravated. He pulled out his phone, turned it on, and saw that Lance had sent several notifications to the group stating that the protest was cancelled. There was an additional message informing that they would meet at the juice bar to regroup and plan a trip to Tallahassee.

"Dang!" said the shorter one. "That is the last time we do a technology fast and a protest bicycle rally at the same time. We totally missed the boat. I wonder why we are going to Tallahassee."

"Tallahassee is the state capital," explained the taller one.

"Why do we have to go there?"

"That is what protesters do. They march on the capitol. The capitol is where you go. Haven't you seen the *Hunger Games*? The capitol is where all the action is. We stick it to the man at the capitol."

"Who is the man?"

"Oh shut up!" said the taller one as they dropped their poster boards and plastic water bottles on the grass and biked away. They had no problem leaving trash on the museum grounds because they were technically anti-Christmas tree protesters. A person can only be true to so many causes.

The florist arrived and asked Dylan to help set up an arch. He was holding a metal rod above his head when Lisa entered the room. He knew his eyesight was not what it used to be, but he thought the caterer looked very much like his old girlfriend. He squinted his eyes while trying to hold the rod steady above his head. A small spider crawled out from its hiding place, stretched its legs, and decided to go for a walk down the rod. It crawled onto Dylan's hand and started making its way down his arm. Dylan threw the rod down, making a loud clattering sound on the floor. The florist gave him a stern look as she picked up the bent rod. He continued to dance around, dusting off his arms trying to make sure the spider was gone. He sheepishly said, "I am sorry. I don't like spiders and snakes."

Lisa naturally looked in the direction of the commotion and was stunned to see her old boyfriend, Dylan Thompson. They stood staring at each other for a few moments in disbelief. Luis walked up to her with an armful of dishes and said, "Where do you want these? Lisa. Lisa! This is heavy and I don't want to hold it all day."

Lisa came back to the present and said in an irritated voice, "Uh, put it … put it … over there. Luis! Figure it out."

Dylan slowly walked up to Lisa and said, "Hello again. It's been the longest time. There has been a lot of water under the bridge."

Lisa regained her composure, drew herself up and said, "Hello, Dylan. It has been a long time. Are you the deejay? Frances Friday must have something to do with this."

"Yes, Frances asked me to fill in as the deejay. That's what friends are for."

The woman who was the subject of their conversation walked into the Pavilion and, seeing the reunited couple, said in a nervous voice, "I see you two are reconnecting. There is nothing like a wedding on a beautiful day with old friends, don't you think so? It is like we are one big happy family."

Dylan had to agree with her, "It's a great day to be alive."

Lady, who had accompanied Frances, said, "Dylan you look a little tired. Are you okay?"

Dylan explained, "Last night, I didn't get to sleep at all. I was trying to get the music just right. Sometimes I go to extremes. But don't worry; you'll be happy."

"We did not give you much time to prepare but I'm sure that it will be amazing," said Frances appreciatively.

"Yes, he's so amazing. He has already dropped the top of the floral arch and dented it," said Lisa, happy to find a criticism of the man who walked out on her.

"Nobody's perfect," said Dylan defending himself.

"I see you still do that thing when you get nervous," said Lisa, annoyed at being spoken to in song titles.

"What thing?" asked Dylan.

"That thing where you use song … never mind. I have work to do and I'm wasting time talking to you. Let's just stay out of each other's way," she said as she turned and walked back toward the kitchen to start the million tasks that had to be completed before the wedding began.

Dylan responded in a defeated voice, "Anything for you." He walked away to resume his duties.

Frances followed Lisa to apologize. "I got here early to tell you that Dylan was hired at the last minute to be the new deejay. It's a long story but the old deejay could not do the job. I recommended Dylan because, you have to admit, he is the best."

"Yes, Dylan is good at everything he does except commitment and relationships," she said bitterly.

"I'm sorry, Lisa," said Frances. "This must be awkward for you. You have to admit that it is a coincidence that you both ended up in the same town. It is like fate brought you together." Frances was hoping that they would blame fate instead of her if the evening did not go well. She was taking a risk bringing these two together again under the same roof. She told herself that some risks were worth taking.

Ignoring fate, Lisa assured her, "No, it will not be awkward. I am a professional and I can do my job well even if Attila the Hun or Adolf Hitler is the deejay. He won't faze me," she said, trying to convince Frances and herself.

"Good," said Frances, hoping Lisa was telling the truth.

Lisa was not telling the truth. Dylan did faze her. She would have to concentrate very hard not to be thinking about him in the background. She was angry that he was the deejay and would make everyone love him and she would be in the background watching. She did not like these negative feelings that were running through her mind and it made her grumpy.

Frances followed her around for a few moments and mustered the courage to say, "I have one more surprise for you. About thirteen of Ella and Auden's friends have come to Palm Beach to attend the wedding uninvited. Do you think you can stretch the food to accommodate them and set up extra tables?"

Lisa took a deep breath and thought before she spoke. If anyone besides Frances had asked her, she would have given a cold answer and pointed out the obvious inconvenience. Instead, she responded, "Well, I did bring extra place settings and some extra food portions. I think I can make that work."

"Fantastic!" said Frances, giving her an appreciative hug.

Luis walked up to the conversation and asked Lisa, "When will the bride get here?"

Lisa, already agitated, shouted at her assistant, "Luis! That is the tenth time you have asked me that question. I don't know when the bride will be here. It'll be later this afternoon. You need to stop asking annoying questions and focus on what you are doing."

As Luis walked away, dejected, Frances looked at Lisa, surprised. "What was that about?"

"Evidently he had a major crush on Ella in high school. He's afraid she won't even remember him. But he doesn't want to ignore her because he thinks that would make him look dumb. He even asked me to make a new name badge that says "assistant caterer" so that he looks more important in her eyes. He's a nervous wreck, but I need him focused."

In Shakespeare's play *Twelfth Night*, the lovesick main character Duke Orsino says, "If music be the food of love, play on. Give me excess of it." Dylan could not stop thinking about Lisa as he was going through the music for the wedding reception. An excess of love songs kept playing on in his brain—love songs that expressed what he would like to say to Lisa. He could not focus on his work as a result.

Unlike Dylan, Lisa was able to focus on her many tasks and momentarily forgot he was working in the background. As her employees put the tablecloths on the round tables, she walked around making sure they fell perfectly to the floor. Crooked tablecloths, in her opinion, were not acceptable for an event on this scale. As she was adjusting one that was slightly uneven, she heard music begin to play through the speakers. As is often the case, the sound of the music is heard before the brain locates and recognizes the melody and then follows with the song title and then the name of the artist. Her brain had identified the song and the name of the artist and the lyrics surfaced in her conscious mind. She heard the familiar words to "Hard to Say I'm Sorry."

She thought it was an odd wedding song but continued with her many tasks. As she unpacked boxes with Luis, she heard another familiar song start to play. This time she made the connection to the song title and artist immediately. Dylan was playing "Always Something There to Remind Me" followed by "Hello."

Luis recognized the song and commented to Lisa, "These don't sound like wedding songs."

"No, they are not!" she agreed. "I think that the deejay is trying to be funny."

The songs continued as Lisa worked. She was picking up the musical theme of a boyfriend who is trying to apologize. This made her angry and happy at the same time. Angry because this was one of the most important days of her career and her old boyfriend seemed to think it was funny to play with her emotions. It made her happy because it seemed that her old boyfriend was thinking about her and was offering a well-deserved apology.

Dylan continued with back to back songs including "Baby Come Back," "Working My Way Back to You," and then "Right Back to Where We Started From." Tasha also noticed the unusual song selections. She shouted across the room to the deejay and said, "What is with this music? Did you do something stupid and need to apologize to your girlfriend? Go tell her you are sorry, then play some better music while we work. This is a wedding not a breakup."

Dylan looked up at Tasha and then at Lisa and shouted back. "You are right. I did do something stupid and I really regret it. Sorry seems to be the hardest word."

Lisa was a mess. Why did this have to happen today? She could not focus on her love life now. She took a deep breath and told herself she would think about her relationship with Dylan later. Almost unconsciously, she grabbed a few appetizers, plated them on a small plate, and told Tasha to take them to the deejay. She remembered the foods Dylan liked and was hoping he would be satisfied with her peace offering until they could have a chance to talk later.

Dylan gladly accepted the gift from Tasha and smiled a hopeful smile. He got back to his deejay tasks and stopped torturing Lisa with the music of his soul.

– Seventeen –
Deidre Decides

DEIDRE SPED TO THE FLAGLER MUSEUM in her convertible Mercedes, taking the turn into the parking lot too fast and screeching her tires. She was alarmed when a homeless man stepped in front of her without looking. She slammed on her brakes. Startled, she jumped out of the car and said, "Are you okay? I did not see you. You should be more careful and look both ways before crossing. You can't just walk in front of moving cars. It could be fatal in this city."

"I'm okay," the man assured her. "I've been through worse," he said in a dejected tone.

Looking at his ragged clothes and dirty face, she said in a sympathetic voice, "Of course you have. I'm sorry that I almost ran over you."

Seeing her kind nature and hearing her sympathetic apology, the homeless man asked her, "Can you spare a few dollars so I can buy my children a loaf of bread?"

"Most certainly not!" said Deidre, outraged. "The worst thing for your children is a loaf of bread. Bread is not good for them, especially white bread! They should eat organic green leafy vegetables and lean farm raised protein. They should also get a good amount of probiotics in their diet and I find herbal teas are very helpful." Forgetting the troubles that caused her to speed to the wedding venue and seeing this man's unfortunate condition compared to hers, Deidre was filled with the milk of human kindness. She rummaged through her oversized purse and found four Whole Foods gift cards she had won at a charity raffle. She handed them to him, "Here, it's only four hundred dollars' worth, but you can buy some very healthy choices for your children with these." She added in a motherly tone, "Do you promise not to buy bread with these?"

The man took the gift cards from Deidre. He thought, "Just my luck! A woman in a Mercedes almost hits me and she does not give me cash but health food store gift cards. I can't catch a break." Still, he was grateful, so he smiled at her and held up two fingers like a boy scout and said, "I promise. I will not buy bread with these."

Deidre was pleased. Following her good deed in the parking lot, she rushed into the building looking for Lisa Moreno. She found her busily instructing her helpers, including Frances and Lady. Without greeting the three women, Deidre launched into a description of the latest wedding crisis, "Another terrible thing has happened! Auden's mother showed me a picture on social media of some of Auden's friends that have driven from North Carolina to come to the wedding. They are not on the guest list. We don't have them in the catering count. I think there are over twenty of them. Oh, I don't know what to do! How am I going to tell Ella and Auden that their friends can't come to the wedding? Now, I am going to have to be the bad person that tells them 'no.' I don't like being the bad person. I don't want to be the bad person. Lady, will you do it? You are good at being harsh."

Lady looked compassionately at her younger sister, who had left the hotel with one false eyelash on and one yet to be applied. Oddly enough, Lady took a remark about being harsh from Deidre as a compliment.

Frances asked, "Why can't they come to the wedding?"

"They were not invited!" said Deidre plainly. "Do you want me to encourage that kind of behavior? They should know better than to come to something uninvited. That is not the kind of surprise people appreciate. It's all very inconvenient."

Frances pointed out, "Yes, they should know better. But they don't. They should not have come, but they did. The question is how do you want this story to be remembered? Do you want to be the hostess that stuck to the rules of etiquette and traditions and turned away their friends? Or, do you want to be remembered as a gracious hostess that welcomed these enthusiastic young people to this beautiful party that you have put together to celebrate your daughter's marriage. They'll remember you forever either way. The choice is up to you. You can embarrass them or you can embrace them. What's it going to be, Deidre?"

John Calvin could have given Deidre advice at this point. He observed that tradition is a good guide but a poor master. Deidre thought for a moment. She did not like the thought of people taking advantage of her hospitality and using poor manners. But then again she liked to think that she was not a slave to tradition for tradition's sake. And she did like the idea of being well-liked by her daughter's friends. She wanted to be remembered as a gracious hostess. She decided to embrace the wedding crashers. Looking at Lisa she said, "We will welcome them with open arms. But how will we feed twenty extra people?"

"Actually, there are only thirteen," said Frances. "Lisa said she could adjust some portions for the dinner and make it work."

"You knew?" said Deidre surprised.

"I got a text from Ella. She spotted one of the wedding crashers at the beauty salon. She did not want to upset you so she asked our advice," Frances explained.

Deidre was relieved. "Well, thank you everyone. I don't know what I would do without my family's help."

During the drive back to The Breakers, Lady asked Frances about the conversation between Lisa and Dylan. "Why did Lisa look so upset with Dylan? It was like they knew each other. Did something else go wrong that you're not telling me about?"

Frances explained, "Dylan and Lisa were engaged at one time, but he left her to go on tour with his band. She is obviously still a little bitter about it. Don't worry. She won't let it get in the way of her job tonight."

"Oh brother!" exclaimed Lady. "We got rid of the deejay that was obsessed with the groom and now we have a caterer and deejay that hate each other. Are all these wedding people connected? Can't we find people to do the wedding that have not dated each other? Is the pool of wedding vendors really so small?"

"I know it's not ideal to have two ex-lovers working at the wedding. Whatever you do, don't tell Deidre or Ella about their relationship. Besides, I don't really think these two hate each other. I think they still have a chance at being together. Didn't you hear all the songs he was playing while we were setting up? I think it's going to be very interesting watching those two tonight. Don't you think it is interesting?"

"Frances, don't get involved, at least not during the wedding."

"I'm not getting involved, I am just thinking."

"I know but when you think, things start happening. Wait until the wedding is over before playing matchmaker."

"I don't think I have to play matchmaker. Somehow, I think the wedding tonight will do it for me."

– Eighteen –
The Ceremony

FLORIDA WAS CREATING AN INSPIRING PAINTING of orange, pink, and light blue pastels as the sun started to sink behind the Flagler Museum. A cool breeze blew as the wedding guests strolled down the colonnade past the coconut grove to the wedding pavilion. Frances and Lady were stationed at the beginning of the colonnade to welcome guests. They greeted platoons of Woods family members as they marched by. They welcomed Thomas and his new friend, Maria, who together slowly made their way to their seats, stopping at every flower arrangement and identifying each by its common as well as Latin name. They welcomed Alexandra, who was walking alone.

"Where is your date?" Lady said with surprise.

Alexandra explained in an irritated voice, "I don't know. He's wandering around the building somewhere. He said he wanted to quickly tour the museum and grounds before taking a seat. He's very strange. Instead of normal conversation, he keeps asking me about our family jewelry and he even wanted to know how my diamond necklace fastened in the back. Aunt Frances, why can't you tell me what is going on and why did you set me up with this weird wedding date?"

"It will all be clear soon," said Frances with a twinkle in her eye. "You can wait for Brick with us."

All three women continued to greet guests. They noticed that Freddie and Trudy were curiously absent. "Where is Freddie?" questioned Lady. "He is always early to parties so he can talk to everyone."

Frances's phone beeped. She showed it to them. "It's Freddie; his text says, 'Help Frances. I need a place to stash the dog.'" They hurried to the parking lot and found Freddie and Trudy waiting by his car.

They looked in disbelief at Trixie-Boo staring up at them from the backseat of Freddie's Audi. "I thought you gave her back today," said Lady.

"Trudy and I tried to make the drop on the way to the wedding," Freddie explained. "We waited over thirty minutes but Lance never showed. I just need to stash the dog until the wedding is over and then we will figure out what to do. We can't leave her in the car."

Looking around, Frances said, "We will have to lock her in the bathroom."

"People will be going in and out of the bathrooms all night," said Lady. "That won't work."

"No, I mean that bathroom," said Frances, pointing to the back of the pavilion. "We will put her in the railcar."

"The railcar?" questioned Alexandra.

"Yes! Henry Flagler's private railcar—Railcar No. 91 is housed in the back of the pavilion," said Frances.

They wrapped Trixie-Boo in Trudy's shawl and quickly dashed from the parking lot into the back of the pavilion and up the steps into the historic railcar. They deposited the dog into the luxurious but small private bathroom. If Trixie-Boo's therapist had been present, he could have told them that closing her in a small bathroom was not a good idea. She suffered from claustrophobic tendencies as well as separation anxiety. Trixie-Boo whimpered loudly and could not be consoled.

Frances said, "Freddie, give her your keys."

"What?" exclaimed Freddie. "Keys to my Audi? What for?"

"She will like chewing on the leather key chain," explained Frances. "Throw your keys in there and let's go."

Freddie tossed his keys into the bathroom and Trudy shut the door. This smell and taste of genuine leather seemed to pacify the little dog, so they left quickly to take their seats.

The van stuffed with Hanlon undergrads careened into the parking lot and took a space at the back of the lot. Arriving late and uninvited to a society wedding in a church van would probably embarrass the average person. However, it did not seem bother any of the undergrads except Graham. As they piled out of the van with wrinkled clothes and messy hair, one undergrad stood apart from the rest. Harley looked like he did not belong to this motley crew. He did not look like he needed to brush his hair. He did not look like he needed anyone to straighten his tie. In fact, no one could have found any way to improve upon his grooming and sartorial choices.

He distanced himself from the undergrad pack, hanging back to mentally prepare himself for the next few hours. He repeated to himself, "Jaunty. Jaunty. Jaunty. I am Cary Grant. I am suave and debonair." He was also contemplating the best way to sit next to Chrissy during the wedding ceremony. He knew that a certain romantic mood came over women at weddings and he wanted to take full advantage of it. He slipped one of the ushers a twenty to seat Chrissy next to him. Once Harley was seated, Chad and Graham tried to sit in the chairs next to him. He said, "I am saving this one for Chrissy. Move over."

Graham at first did not want to move. However, the light started to dawn on Chad. First there was Harley's mysterious makeover. Then Harley's new clothes and now he was saving a seat for Chrissy. It all became clear to Chad. Harley was into Chrissy. He smiled a goofy smile, punched Harley in the shoulder and said "Dude" multiple times. He pushed Graham to the next chair and sat down, leaving a space for her.

Within a few minutes, Chrissy was seated next to Harley. At first she thought a random guest had been seated among the Hanlon pack. She did a double take when she realized who was seated next to her and she said in a loud voice, "Harley?"

Harley's heart was pounding like those thingamajigs that drive pylons into the foundation of a building. He regained his composure, took a deep breath, and said in a debonair voice, "Good evening Chrissy. You look lovely."

Chrissy did not know where to begin. She had so many questions. When and where did he get his haircut? Who groomed his beard and mustache? Who gave him the finely tailored clothes and Italian shoes? What was the alluring cologne he was wearing?

The wedding ceremony was beginning, as signaled by the change in the music. She did not have time to quiz him, so she just said, "Thank you Harley." And she sat back in her chair.

Ministrix Beatrix, the groom, and the groomsmen filed in and stood at the front as the processional began. The plan to surprise the groom by showing up to his wedding unannounced was a success. Auden's reaction was mixed at first, but his bewilderment melted into good feelings and he gave a big smile and nodded his head in the direction of his little rat pack. He was very touched that they would make time to be a part of his big day. Chad and Graham smiled and waved at Auden like little children in the school play waving at their parents. In contrast, Harley did not smile and wave but ever so slightly lifted his chin in acknowledgement of the groom's glance in his direction.

Ella appeared in the aisle with her father, Max. She was smiling from ear to ear. This was her big moment and she was enjoying every minute. She had chosen a vintage blush-colored dress instead of the traditional white. The gown was overlaid with an intricate lace on the bodice and down the sides. The tulle fabric kicked out at the bottom not quite like a mermaid, but not a full ball gown. The lace-covered cap sleeves had a double row of pearls that draped along the edge with one large pearl pendant that hung in the middle of her arm. Around her neck, she wore her grandmother's pearls in double strands that hung almost to her waistline. She also wore multiple pearl bracelets of different sizes on both wrists. Her nails were a perfect pearlescent color. Her extra large bouquet was a mixture of off-white and light pink roses with strands of waterfall crystals and pearls dangling from it. Her custom headpiece was a pink velvet head-band covered to the edges with vintage-looking crystals and pearls in kind of an acanthus leaf pattern. On either side of the band were cascades of pearls that were placed to hang down at her temples.

An audible, "Oh!" was heard as the wedding guests saw the bride. The crowd was also moved by watching the bride's father bravely trying to hold back the tears that were beginning to form in the corners of his eyes. He was normally a jovial man who cracked jokes and was never very serious, but today he was trying hard not to bawl his eyes out. The reality of this event had finally crashed in on him. It was all going to change and there was no doubt about it; it was bittersweet for him. He had prepared for everything in this wedding except his own emotions.

The bride's father was not the only man who had not prepared emotionally for this moment. The groom's face showed a mixture of panic and disorientation as his bride approached. To the crowd, Auden looked like a man who was helplessly facing a grizzly bear charging down the aisle toward him. He felt his throat tighten and his eyes begin to well up. All at once, a feeling of maturity washed over him like coruscations of light from above, and he could swear he felt his spine straighten a little. He did not feel like an irresponsible college student anymore. He felt like a real man, and the woman he was lucky enough to marry was coming down the aisle. Added to this mature state of mind was the feeling of love and support from his family, and now his rat pack, present in the audience. This caused him to think deeply about life for the first time.

A family friend corralled the flower girl and ring bearer at the back of the pavilion. To occupy them she let them climb into the railcar until it was their turn to walk down the aisle. She noticed the ring bearer was pre-occupied by something in the bathroom. She thought she heard a jingling sound but did not see the small dog hiding behind the toilet. She took the children each by hand and walked down the railcar steps, leaving the bathroom door open.

The adorable children toddled down the aisle in their fussy wedding outfits as an audible "Aww" was heard. This wedding had an added bonus for the guests' enjoyment—a Pekingese dog. Trixie-Boo followed the children out of the railcar and down the aisle, stepping in time with the music. Being a well-bred show dog, she innately sensed the decorum necessary for the occasion. She held her head high as she jingled Freddie's key chain in her mouth.

Ella recognized her ex-aunt's show dog and thought it was a gift from her Uncle Freddie. As Trixie-Boo took her place among the bridesmaids, the crowd smiled with delight and Ella was thrilled. She thought, "What a wonderful wedding gift," and she beamed at her uncle in the crowd. Freddie smiled back uneasily.

Ministrix Beatrix began the ceremony by welcoming the guests. "Welcome friends and family to this most happy occasion. We are here today for the unification of the hearts of Allen—"

Auden corrected the ministrix. "Auden," he said loudly.

"Of course, Auden and this lovely young lady, Ellen."

"Ella!" the bride corrected.

"Yes, of course, Ella. What is a name? It is a mere title we carry through life, but not our true essence. No matter what these two young people are named, anyone present can tell that the stars have brought them together. United they stand, er, uh divided they fall."

The ministrix had never owned a pet and did not realize that some people are highly allergic to animal dander. She was about to discover that she was one of those people. As she began to address the young couple, a tickle started in her upper nostril and traveled down her sinus cavity, causing her eyes to water and her nose to run. She began the vows with, "Au, Au, Au, Achoo! Auden. Do you take this woman to be your wife?"

Auden responded that he did.

She continued, "And, Eh, Eh, Echoo! Ella do you take this ma, ma, maaachoo! Man to be your husband?"

Ella responded that she did.

Trixie-Boo was intrigued by the sneezing sound and moved in to get a closer look, pushing herself in between the bride and groom. This caused the ministrix to begin a non-stop sneezing fit and she dropped her leather bound notebook. Trixie-Boo seized the notebook in her small mouth and ran down the aisle and outside as if she had captured a treasure. Alexandra was amused at first, but her smile turned to shock as her date jumped up and followed the dog outside. She thought, "Of course that is what a weird person would do—jump up in the middle of the ceremony and follow a dog out." She scowled at her Aunt Frances, who just smiled and shrugged her shoulders.

The ministrix, without her notebook, was at a loss for what to say next. She mumbled some more wedding-sounding mumbo jumbo and finally said, "Now the bride and groom will exchange their personally written vows for our eh, ur, enjoyment."

She stepped to the side and the bride and groom faced each other and held hands. Auden began.

Ladies in the audience, including Chrissy, fished in their purses for a tissue when they heard the groom's voice crack while reciting his vows. Harley, on Guy's suggestion, had a cotton handkerchief handy for her use. He handed it to her with a smile. She quietly mouthed the words "thank you" as she took the handkerchief. Dabbing her eyes, she thought, "Who is this guy and what has he done with Harley?"

Freddie, who was accustomed to hearing wedding vows, was touched by the ceremony, and as a result a few small tears rolled down his check. Trudy handed him a tissue from the packet that she had pulled out of her purse to dry her own tears.

Thomas did not shed any tears because he was deep in thought. He recognized the Pekingese dog that had just run down the aisle, but he could not remember where he had seen her. He also was sure he had spoken to the ministrix before but could not place her either. His mind was incapable of handling so many questions at once, so he tuned back into the ceremony just as the ministrix said, "I now pronounce them husband and wife."

– Nineteen –
The Reception

THE WEDDING PARTY PROCEEDED and the wedding guests filed out onto the terrace for the cocktail reception. Lisa the caterer and Dylan the deejay were now in charge of the evening. Lisa's servers provided the guests with hors d'oeuvre and drinks as they mingled and talked. Luis and the other servers glided around the terrace like choreographed dancers refreshing the guests with delicious appetizers. Tasha was at the open bar monitoring the amount of alcohol the uninvited Hanlon undergrads imbibed. Dylan played mingling music in the background and monitored the status of the wedding party, who were being photographed.

Brick found Alexandra standing with her father and Maria. He did not have time to explain his behavior during the ceremony to Alexandra. Her father interrupted him midsentence with a suspicious tone in his voice and his best fatherly expression on his face. "This must be Brick," he said extending his hand and giving an extra firm handshake. "Is that your first or last name, or a nickname, maybe?"

"Brick is my first name. Nice to meet you, Mr.

Friday," said Brick, extending his hand with an equally firm grip.

Thomas shook the substantial hand. "You can call me Mr. Friday," he said in an authoritative tone. He looked up at the young man's face and asked his daughter in a concerned voice, "Where did you meet this Brick?"

"In a store," she answered.

"In a store?" Thomas said, a little confused.

"Yes, on Worth Avenue," she said, not giving too much detail.

"On Worth Avenue?" Thomas repeated.

"Yes, he was walking his dog and I tripped and we met."

"He was walking his dog and you tripped and met?"

"Yes!" said Alexandra getting annoyed at her father's parrot routine. "Aunt Frances knows him."

"Your Aunt Frances knows him?" said Thomas.

"Yes, Father!" said Alexandra, stopping her dad short. She turned her attention to Brick. "Why did you get up during the ceremony and chase the dog?"

"I wanted to make sure she was okay. She looked distressed. I was concerned that she would eat some of the food or chew up the notebook or maybe fall in the water. I am still worried. I looked everywhere and can't find her."

Alexandra was temporarily satisfied with this answer since Brick did own a border collie. Maybe he was one of those men who really connected with dogs. Maybe he was a big, strong, sensitive, animal loving type. One thing was certain; her date was a puzzle and she was determined to figure him out by the night's end.

After the wedding pictures, Ella changed into her reception dress. When shopping for her wedding dress she had debated whether to buy just one dress or two for her big day. She wondered, "Would it take too long to change? Are two dresses really necessary?" But, given the chance to buy two fabulous, once-in-a-lifetime dresses, she decided to just do it. In keeping with her theme, her reception dress was not unlike a dress that Daisy Buchanan would wear to a party thrown by Gatsby.

It was more comfortable and fit for dancing. She kept her headpiece on but switched her grandmother's long double string of pearls for another beautiful piece that was more of a choker made of four strands of pearls with a diamond pendant in the front. She also took off a couple of pearl bracelets and tossed them in a bag with the other jewelry. She put on an arm cuff, also laden with pearls and crystals.

Getting the signal that the bride was ready, Dylan notified the guests that the cocktail reception was coming to a close, and he directed them to enter the West Room for the reception and take their seats at the assigned tables. Of course what he actually said was, "Move along, move along. Walk it out to the reception. I know you are having the time of your life, but you ain't seen nothing yet."

The guests were seated in the Mediterranean-themed West Room. The wrought iron grand chandelier hanging from the vaulted ceiling and the wall sconces lit the room so that it looked almost enchanted. All eyes were on the stairs leading into the West Room and all hands were clapping as the wedding party was introduced.

Dylan had observed over many years as a deejay that the ability to dance was randomly scattered among the population. It was his custom to play a fast-paced song to make the bridal party entrance quicker and less painful for the members not blessed with the gift of dance. As each bridesmaid and groomsman was introduced, they performed the obligatory funky dance-walk into the reception.

Each person had his or her own signature moves. The first bridesmaid opted for the exaggerated hip swing walk with her bouquet in the air. The first groomsman did a spin and jazz hands combo. Most couples chose the safe option of shooting gun hands and mouth open move. The less experienced wedding walkers opted for the simple Olympic platform raised hands move. None of these moves could compete with the ring bearer and the flower girl, who thought they were in a field day race and ran into the room like scared rabbits.

The bride and groom entered the room, stopped in the spotlight, and did a brief twirl and dip foreshadowing things to come. They sparkled and shone in the light like a model couple that anyone would be happy to follow on

Instagram. After they enjoyed dinner and a few toasts, the guests were in for a treat, as Ella and Auden had prepared a special first dance.

Hours before the wedding, Dylan changed the first dance song to one he thought was more appropriate for the couple.

When she saw the song change, Ella texted Dylan, "Is this song legit?"

Dylan texted back, "Trust me. Would I lie to you?"

The designated cameras were ready to record a YouTube-worthy first dance as Dylan began playing "With This Ring" by the Platters. Ella's dress twisted, twirled and sparkled with each triple step and spin. At Hanlon, they had won the spring shag dance competition, so they performed the dance to perfection. With the last twirl and dip the wedding guests showed their approval with a standing ovation. Max, Ella's father was wiping more tears from his eyes as pride for his daughter beamed on his face. He thought during this very memorable moment, the thousands of dollars he had spent for his daughter's private college education had been worth every penny.

In a Hollywood movie depicting a wedding reception, the viewer often gets a montage of the movements of the main characters as well as vignettes of short conversations. This gives an overview of the wedding reception and avoids a boring detailed account of every minute of the five-hour event. This is an effective tool to relate what happened the evening of the Birnam-Woods wedding reception.

When Dylan played "I've Got the World on a String," Freddie extended his hand to Grandma Ethel and said, "Come on, old woman. Let's dance." Halfway through the song, Ethel said the bunion on her foot was hurting and she suggested that Freddie continue the dance with Trudy. Freddie twirled Ethel over to the table and scooped up Trudy to finish the dance. Trudy was hesitant at first, but then jumped up and eagerly grabbed Freddie's hand.

"I'm not much of a dancer," she said self-consciously. Trudy was normally very confident, but Freddie was the most outgoing, attractive man that had ever asked her to dance. This was new territory for her.

"Of course you are!" said Freddie. "You're doing great. I'm surprised at you, Trudy, saying self-limiting statements like that. You seem to be good at everything you do!"

"Thanks, Freddie," said Trudy. "I wish I had your confidence. Don't you ever feel self-conscious or timid or unsure of yourself?"

"Never!" said Freddie. "Besides, what do you need my confidence for? You are a beautiful, intelligent, successful woman." Even though Freddie's personality tended to err toward flattery, he actually meant these words. He was a little surprised how easily they rolled off his lips, but he thought, "It is true, and it is about time someone told her these things."

Some wedding guests approached Dylan, who was stationed at the deejay table overlooking the room. They suggested that he play the hokey pokey, the chicken dance or the Macarena because, as they put it, "that is what you play at weddings." He was insulted by their suggestions and answered sarcastically, "So you think anything I can do you can do better. I know you want to express yourself but, dream on," indicating that under no circumstances would he be playing those songs tonight.

When Dylan played "We are Family," Brick noticed that Ministrix Beatrix left her table and was climbing the short staircase into the hallway. He jumped up from the table suddenly. Alexandra put a hand on his coat sleeve and asked, "Where are you going now?"

Brick stammered and then said, "I am, I am, am going to ask the ministrix to dance."

Alexandra thought this was odd. Her date had not shown any indication that he wanted to dance so she categorized him as a non-dancer. Now he was going to ask an older woman to dance. Maybe he preferred full-figured, spiritual women to someone like her. She moved her hand from his sleeve and said, "Uh, okay."

Brick followed the ministrix up the stairs and down the hallway. She was headed for the back room that Ella had used as a changing room. Trixie-Boo came out from her hiding spot and also decided to follow the mysterious ministrix. After leaving the ceremony with notebook in mouth, the intelligent pup had successfully outmaneuvered Brick. Unfortunately, she dropped the notebook but avoided capture by hiding quietly behind a potted palm. Becoming bored with hiding, she joined Brick in tailing the ministrix.

Alexandra decided to follow Brick, but a random

wedding guest tapped her shoulder and asked her to dance. As she danced with Steve, as he had introduced himself, she slowly moved closer to the stairwell where Brick had exited the room. She was looking over her short dance partner, scanning the hallway looking for Brick. Steve asked, "Are you a friend of the bride or groom?"

Alexandra was not particularly interested in conversation but answered, "I'm the bride's cousin. What about you?"

The stranger said, "I'm a friend of the bride also. We went to high school together. We actually dated at one time but it did not work out. Of course, I broke up with her."

"Oh?" said Alexandra, mildly interested. The song ended and everyone turned to hear Dylan's announcement that the single ladies should take to the dance floor. Alexandra turned back to thank her dance partner, but he had vanished.

Luis was taking a break from his duties and was observing the wedding reception. Leaning on the iron railing overlooking the dance floor he had overheard Alexandra's conversation with Steve. Luis had exceptionally good hearing and, had he not chosen a career in culinary arts, could have pursued a career as a private investigator. His natural curiosity and powers of observation were put to good use at this moment. The stranger dancing with Alexandra had most certainly not dated Ella Birnam in high school. Luis could easily make a list of Ella's high school boyfriends and, on top of that, he did not recognize "Steve" as one of his school's alumni. He decided to follow him.

When Dylan played "Single Ladies," Frances found Alexandra standing at the edge of the dance floor half dancing and half looking around the room. She smiled at her lovely niece and then suddenly gasped, "Alexandra! Where is your necklace?"

Alexandra felt her neck, looked down at her dress and said, "I don't know. I had it on during dinner. How could I lose it?"

Frances said, "Let's retrace your steps." They worked their way back to the table, scanning the floor for anything that sparkled. Frances also began scanning the room for any sign of Brick or the ministrix. She was worried.

When Dylan played "Talking Out Loud," Harley knew this was the perfect moment to ask Chrissy to dance. Earlier in the afternoon, the bridesmaid that was CIA material ducked into the reception hall and moved the seat assignments around to ensure that Harley and Chrissy were seated next to each other at the same table. Harley turned to Chrissy and said, "Chrissy, may I have—" he broke off as he noticed Chrissy stand and walk to the dance floor with one of the Woods cousins.

Chad noticed and said, "Dude! That guy just stole your dance."

"Where did he come from?" said Harley. "How many cousins do Ella and Auden have? These pesky cousins are coming out of the woodwork." Harley was unprepared for this. What should he do? Chrissy did not really owe him anything, but why did she accept this other dude so quickly? He did not have much time. He wanted to dance to this song. His hairdresser's words came back to him, "Jaunty. Be jaunty." What would a debonair, jaunty man do? Remembering an old Cary Grant movie, he decided to cut in on their dance. He walked up to the dancing couple, tapped the interfering cousin on the shoulder and said, "May I cut in?"

At first, the Woods cousin wanted to say, "Get lost, loser," but the dignified surroundings and the determined look on Harley's face caused him to nod and step aside and off the dance floor. Harley danced with Chrissy in a jaunty mood and they talked about the beautiful wedding and how glad they were that they took the road trip.

Frances accidentally bumped into Harley. "Excuse me," she said. "We are looking for a lost piece of jewelry. Are you two having a good time?"

They both answered that they were having a great time.

Chrissy whispered to Harley, "Ella's whole family have been so nice to us even though we showed up at the last minute, uninvited. They had a table for us with place cards and everything. I am so impressed."

"I know," agreed Harley. "They are really nice. I'm happy Auden is marrying into such a nice family." He watched them hunt for Alexandra's necklace and said, "Maybe we should help them look."

Feeling very proud of her friend, Chrissy smiled and said, "Yes, Harley that would be a very nice thing to do. Let's help them."

When Dylan played "Footloose," Thomas took

Maria's hand and led her to the dance floor. To say that Thomas Friday could not dance would be the understatement of the century. If his dancing were described as the cross between a baby giraffe learning to walk and a toddler waiting to go potty, it would be a kind description. As David says in the Psalms, "who can discern his own errors," Thomas Friday did not know that he could not dance. He was just excited to be holding Maria in his arms and dancing.

As he twirled her around, it reminded her of being at an ice-skating rink as a child and playing whiplash. His twirling was more like flinging but Thomas seemed to be having a good time, and she was going to reach her daily fitness goal, so she did not mind. The single women in the crowd that had hopes of meeting the wealthy, available Thomas Friday sighed a sigh of both disappointment and relief: disappointment that he brought a date and relief that they were not his dance partners.

When Dylan played "September," Brick was knocking on the door of the back room. He had lost track of the ministrix and he deduced that this was the only place she could be hiding. No one answered, but he was sure he heard movement in the room. He slowly opened the door. He found the ministrix sitting in a chair with a glass of water and fanning her face with a wedding program.

"Hello," she said. "I needed some quiet time to myself. Performing a wedding drains me of all my emotional energy. Can I help you? Are you lost, young man?"

Brick scanned the room and all its contents and did not answer her right away.

The ministrix, trying to be sensitive to a seeking soul, said, "Perhaps you need spiritual advice. I can give you my card and we can set something up. As you can see, my cup has been drained this evening and I have to replenish the well of my knowledge before I can give it out again."

Brick wanted to get the ministrix out of the room. He stammered, "Uh, I was going to ask you to dance. Would you like to dance?"

"No, thank you. I will just sit here and enjoy the solitude. Close the door on your way out," said the ministrix, getting annoyed at his intrusion.

Brick was trying to think of another plan when Trixie-Boo bounded into the room and began barking at the ministrix. Although she was not a hunting dog breed, she was thrilled that she and Brick had cornered their prey. In her life as a show dog, she could not remember a weekend filled with so much fun and excitement. She continued barking and jumped up with her tiny legs pushing off the ministrix's chair.

The ministrix tried to swat the dog away but her nose began another sneezing fit. She jumped up, pushed a chair towards Brick, and ran out of the room, slamming the door behind her. The chair hit Brick's knee exactly in the spot of an old football injury, so he ran-limped after her. Trixie-Boo was thrilled to continue the chase and she did not diminish her barking as she took off after Brick.

Most wedding planners are shortsighted and lack the necessary creativity to include a chase scene during a wedding reception as a way to liven things up. If they had noticed the long hallways elevated six feet above and encircling the West room, perhaps they could have envisioned it. While Dylan was playing "I Got A Feeling," the Birnam-Woods wedding guests were treated to such a chase scene. The ministrix ran down the hallway, holding up her long robe to avoid tripping, only stopping at intervals to sneeze. An athletic young man was limping along after her and in turn was being chased by a yapping Pekingese dog. Who wants a run-of-the-mill wedding reception when you can have this kind of exhibition? Many future brides and their mothers in the crowd jotted down the idea.

Frances, Lady, and Alexandra stopped looking for the necklace and followed the chase towards the Great Hall. They did not find Brick or the ministrix or the dog but what they did find was Luis crouching under a window peeping out into the courtyard. They all crouched down and Frances said in a whisper, "Luis, what are you doing here? What are you looking at?"

Luis whispered his answer, "I have been following one of the guests. He said he dated Ella in high school, so I followed him."

"Luis, you are taking this obsession with Ella too far," Frances protested in a loud voice.

"Shhh," he said quieting her. Pointing toward the courtyard he said, "This guy is not who he says he is. He has been hiding in those palms and when he saw you coming he dropped something in the fountain and jumped back into the bushes."

Freddie and Trudy, who had also seen the recently kidnapped dog in the chase, came and crouched down behind the group. Freddie said in a whisper that startled the rest of them, "What are we doing? Did you find the Peke?"

Frances answered, "No, Freddie. We are watching a wedding guest who just put something in the fountain."

"Maybe it was a penny. Maybe he did it for good luck," noted Freddie.

Lady was tired of this nonsense and wanted to get back to her niece's wedding. She straightened up and stopped whispering. "Frances what is going on? Why did the ministrix run out of the reception?"

Alexandra straightened up and added, "And why was my wedding date chasing her?"

And Freddie, not wanting to be left out of the questioning, straightened up and joined in, "And how did Trixie-Boo get out of the railcar?"

They all peered at Frances, but she did not have a chance to explain. Steve, hearing the commotion, popped out of the bushes and ran for the front entrance. Alexandra shouted, "There he goes!"

Frances shouted, "Luis! Get him!"

Luis, who was a state track and field champion, chased Steve. They ran in and out of the palm trees lining the front lawn like two dogs racing through an agility course. But Luis's ability to make tight turns and his speed enabled him to close the gap. He caught up to Steve, tackled him, and held him down on the ground.

Thomas and Maria wanted to get some fresh air and take a break from dancing. They meandered into the courtyard and were delighted to find another assortment of plants to admire and discuss. Thomas reflected, "Ah, this is a nice courtyard. You know they designed houses with courtyards like this to give ample lighting to all the rooms. Also, it helps keep the house cool by allowing the ocean breezes to cross ventilate the house."

Maria nodded and said, "What a beautiful fountain. The water sounds so peaceful."

"That is a copy of a fountain in Florence. It is Venus, the goddess of love," Thomas added, trying to sound romantic.

They moved closer to the beautifully lit fountain that was spilling water in a rhythmic sound. Thomas noticed the water shimmering. It shimmered and sparkled more than fountain water, in his experience, was supposed to shimmer and sparkle. He said to Maria, "I think there is something in the bottom of the fountain." He rolled up his sleeve, reached into the water and drew out a diamond necklace. Maria was startled. She had only known Thomas a few days and now he was giving her jewelry—elaborate, expensive, diamond jewelry. She started to protest and say she could not possibly accept such a gift when Thomas said, "This looks like my daughter's necklace. What the devil is it doing at the bottom of the fountain?" Maria was more relieved than disappointed that the necklace was not a gift for her.

Brick walked back onto the lawn in front of the Flagler Museum accompanied by Ministrix Beatrix on one side and Trixie-Boo under his arm on the other. The ministrix's hands were handcuffed behind her back, and Trixie-Boo growled at her now and then. One thing that got her hackles up was a jewelry thief. Two men who appeared to be officers of the law accompanied them. He bent over Luis, who was holding Steve on the grass, and said, "Good work. We will take it from here."

Alexandra, Freddie, Trudy, Luis, and Lady were stunned. They stood with mouths gaping open watching the ministrix and Steve being arrested. Frances, however, did not look surprised. They all noticed Frances smiling and Lady said, "You knew about this?"

"Yes," said Frances. "Brick enlisted my help that day we saw him shopping. He had a feeling that there would be an attempted robbery tonight."

"You did not tell anyone? Weren't you taking quite a risk? What if the thieves had gotten away?" questioned Lady.

Frances had not really thought about the risk or if they were not successful. She was confident that they could catch the thieves. She said, "I guess it was kind of risky, but we caught them and it all turned out well."

Deidre came running out of the museum towards them. She was screaming with her hands flailing above her head, "Frances, Lady, Freddie! Someone has stolen Ella's jewelry from the changing room. I was packing up her things getting her ready to go and we can't find the pearls anywhere. Oh, someone has taken our family heir-looms. What should we do?"

She stopped running and shouting and halted with a perplexed look on her face. She said, "What are you all doing out here?" She joined the group of stunned observers and her mouth gaped open as well.

Brick stepped forward to calm Deidre. He extended his hand, opened his palm and said, "You mean these pearls?" Deidre looked from the pearls to Brick's face and back again. Brick, sensing that an explanation was necessary, said in an official tone, "Everyone, this is Aunt Bea of the infamous Silver Spoon Gang and her accomplice Charlie Potts. They came to your wedding with the intention of stealing your jewelry and anything else they could get their hands on."

Deidre said, "No, that is not Aunt Bea; that is my old high school chum Ministrix Beatrix. She just officiated my daughter's wedding. There must be some mistake."

Lady explained, "Deidre, don't you get it? Bea tricked you into letting her officiate the wedding. She probably overheard you in the hotel lobby panicking about not having a minister. It wasn't the universe answering your call; it was a con artist waiting for an opportunity."

Bea gritted her teeth and growled at her accomplice Charlie, "You was supposed to keep these people off my back so I could lift the jewelry. You idiot, you didn't wait for my signal to take the necklace either. You bonehead. I oughta …" The two officers separated Bea and Charlie and stuffed them into police cars and drove away.

Brick continued, "We heard some chatter and suspected that this gang would pull another heist at a society wedding this month. I was assigned to your wedding to be on the lookout for an attempted robbery. Luckily, I got Bea's fingerprints off the notebook that this little doggy picked up." He scratched Trixie-Boo's ears. "I was able to immediately identify her."

The proud Peke licked Brick's nose as if to say, "It was the least I could do. Glad to help. I am available anytime."

Brick looked at Frances and said, "I appreciate your help, Frances, in not giving away my cover. We couldn't have caught the thieves without your discretion and help."

"You are quite welcome, Brick, or whatever your real name is," said Frances.

Alexandra questioned, "What is your real name?"

Brick stammered. "My name is not important. The important thing is that your family jewelry was recovered and everyone is safe."

Alexandra exclaimed, "Oh my gosh, I forgot about my necklace. Steve, I mean Charlie probably took it and put it in the fountain."

They all dashed back to the courtyard, followed by Trixie-Boo, but they did not find a necklace in the fountain. As they started to search the courtyard area, Thomas and Maria stepped out from behind the landscaping. Thomas said to the group, "We were uh, examining the banana trees. I don't think they are quite ripe yet. Isn't that right, Maria?" Maria blushed and agreed. Thomas turned his attention to Alexandra and held out his hand containing the diamond necklace and said in a fatherly tone, "Now look here, young lady. If you can't keep your mother's diamond necklace out of fountains, I am not going to let you wear it."

Alexandra explained, "A thief stole my necklace and put it in the fountain. I am so relieved you found it." She took it and put it around her neck with Brick's assistance.

Thomas continued the lecture. "Well that is because you probably left it sitting around somewhere for the thief to take. I have always told you to not leave your things lying about."

Frances interjected, "Thomas, the ministrix and one of the guests are jewel thieves who were trying to rob us. Luckily they were caught by Alexandra's date."

Thomas was astonished. "The ministrix? What has become of the clergy these days? If they can't be trusted whom can we trust?"

Lady said, "Thomas, she was not a real minister; she was a con artist and a thief."

Thomas said, "I thought there was something suspicious about that woman." His face brightened. "Now I remember! I met someone just like her in the lobby, although she had blonde hair. She said she was an international jewelry designer. We had a nice chat and I told her all about our family heirloom jewelry. She seemed very interested. Do you think she was the same woman as the ministrix?"

Lady rolled her eyes and said, "Well, now we know why the Silver Spoon Gang chose our wedding. Thomas inventoried our priceless jewelry for them and Deidre invited the gang leader to the wedding."

Frances interjected, "Now that that is over, let's get back to the wedding reception and enjoy ourselves."

When Dylan played "Good Time," Ella walked over to Luis and asked him to dance. Luis blushed from head to toe, took her outstretched hand and followed the bride onto the dance floor. She said, "My Aunt Frances tells me that you tackled the thief and helped save our family heirloom jewelry."

"It was nothing," gushed Luis. "You probably remember that I ran track in high school." He smiled and said proudly, "The guy didn't have a chance."

"I remember," said Ella. "You are a hero!" She smiled at her former classmate. "I asked Dylan to play this song. Do you remember it?"

"Yes," said Luis. "It is our senior class song."

They danced and talked about their high school days saying, "Do you remember old so-and-so who taught math" and "remember when we won that state football game." Good times. When Luis explained what his plans for his life were, Ella responded, "That is so cool." When Ella explained that she did not have any immediate goals for her future, Luis responded, "That is cool too."

Frances watched Luis and Ella dance. She thought that Luis looked different. In addition to wearing a giant smile for the first time, he seemed taller, more confident, more like a mature man. Frances's observation was correct. Luis felt like an old chapter was ending and a new chapter was beginning. He had been validated by his high school crush. He could now put away childish things and look forward to a future full of possibilities.

As Dylan played "All of Me," Alexandra danced for the first time with her wedding date. The recent events had completely erased any suspicions she had about this odd young man and she was now enjoying herself. While they were dancing close, she asked, "Tell me your real name?"

Brick sighed, "You will laugh if I tell you."

"No, I will not laugh. I promise. Tell me your name," she whispered softly.

"My real name is Robin Banks. My friends call me Rob. There, now you know!" he said, exasperated.

"Robbing Banks! That is not your real name!" she said as she pulled away from him. "If you can't be serious, this date is over. Just tell me the truth!"

"Not Robbing Banks. Robin Banks is my real name. Honest." He produced his badge to prove it.

Alexandra did not keep her promise not to laugh. She said, giggling, "You work for the police and your name is Rob Banks, ah, ha, ha … I am sorry, it is just so funny."

Rob clarified, "Actually, I work for the FBI. I am glad you are so amused."

The song ended and Dylan started playing "Brown Eyed Girl." Rob felt a tap on his shoulder. Thomas wanted to dance with his daughter. Despite his awkward, jerking dance moves, dancing with her father was one of the highlights of her evening. She was starting to appreciate her father for the first time, and she was excited to begin this new chapter of their relationship. She was filled with that same overwhelming feeling of happiness that kept breaking in on her the whole weekend.

As Dylan played a compilation of songs from *Grease*, the couple's favorite musical, he announced that the bride and groom would be leaving soon. The wedding guests slowly made their way to the museum entrance with sparklers in hand. They held their sparklers high in the air and tossed silver streamers as the newlyweds hurried toward the car. The music could still be heard as Ella and Auden drove away in a white Rolls Royce.

– Twenty –
The Day After Denouement

THE MEMBERS OF THE FRIDAY FAMILY did not take advantage of the sumptuous Sunday buffet at The Breakers, having been well fed the previous night by Lisa Moreno's catering. Instead they chose to meet for a quick coffee and pastry before traveling back to their various homes. Deidre and Max, although exhausted from months of planning their daughter's society wedding, decided to meet with their family one more time.

Frances remarked, "Deidre, despite all the challenges, that was the most beautiful, enjoyable, and exciting wedding I have ever been to—and I have been to many. It turned out really well."

Deidre beamed. "Thank you! I am very pleased at how everything turned out. I had so many compliments from my friends saying it was the most unique wedding they had ever attended. That is exactly what I was going for—unique." She looked around at each family member present and added, "And I appreciate everyone's help in making Ella and Auden's wedding a success. Cheers!"

They clinked coffee cups and Deidre turned to her

brother Sam. "I am so glad that you made it to the wedding in time although I wish you could have been here earlier. I don't know what we would have done if you hadn't reached out to your friend the judge so that he could officially marry them before they got on the plane this morning." Turning to the rest of the family, she explained, "The minstrix was not licensed to perform weddings. Can you believe it? It really is a shame because she was such a magnetic person. I was inspired by the things she said."

Lady interjected, "Deidre she was not really a spiritual person; she was a crook. You realize the difference, don't you?"

Thomas chimed in and stated the obvious. "I couldn't understand a word she said. None of it made any sense. Stars and poems and violin strings, it was all stuff and nonsense. If you ask me, she was a complete phony."

Deidre answered, "I know she lied to us and tried to steal our jewelry but you have to agree that she had a knack for giving spiritual advice. It is too bad she is a criminal. I wonder if she could still give me advice from prison."

"Advice? Why do you feel you need advice?" asked Frances.

Deidre became a little melancholy. "I'm really going to miss having Ella living at home and I'm afraid that I might slip into a depression. I may need to see a counselor. I am not going to handle it as well as you and Lady did."

Lady interjected her realistic viewpoint. "Ella was

away four years at college and you only saw her on breaks so there has been some separation already. Besides, Ella and Auden will be living two houses down in the house you bought for them and, at this point, they do not have jobs, so I think you will not feel the effects as severely as some families."

"I suppose you are right. Still. It is not the same," said Deidre wistfully.

Sam felt compassion for his little sister and so he offered a suggestion. "Deidre, would you like to house an exchange student in the spring? I only ask because I have a few clients with teenagers who have nowhere to stay. The company that arranged their exchange went out of business and left them stranded and did not give their money back. Maybe helping someone will take your mind off your empty nest."

Deidre thought about it. "That sounds intriguing. Could I get a blonde girl, about five foot four who likes to shop?"

Frances explained, "It does not work that way Deidre. You can't pick them. I think you should do it. You would be a wonderful hostess and you have such a big heart and plenty of room at your house. Sam and I are hosting a teenage boy from France."

Lady chimed in, "I want to host someone. My house is empty too. Can I have a person from England? You know I love all things English. We would have so much in common already."

Sam was pleased at his siblings' generous response and said, "I will see what I can do."

Freddie strolled in and took a seat next to his brother Sam. After placing his order, he sipped his water, put his napkin in his lap. When he looked up he noticed Frances, Lady, and Deidre smiling oddly at him. He leaned over to Sam and whispered, "Why are they staring at me with strange looks on their faces?"

Sam looked at them and considered. He whispered back, "Did you do something stupid this weekend that you want to tell me about Freddie?"

"Nothing more than the usual. They don't look angry. It looks more like they are happy that I did something right."

"And look!" said Sam. "It is spreading." Alexandra was smiling at Freddie, as were her cousins Fallon, Farryn, Faith, and Victoria. The remaining Friday family women had arrived just before the ceremony. They had heard all about the excitement leading up to the wedding, including stories about Uncle Freddie.

"All the Friday women are smiling at you," said Sam as he pointed down the line of women at the breakfast table.

Frances acted as the spokesperson for the group. She said, "Freddie, did you enjoy the weekend?"

"Of course I did, Frances. I enjoy every weekend. The wedding was spectacular."

Frances clarified, "I mean did you enjoy spending time with any particular person this weekend?"

"I love spending time with my family. I love seeing my brothers and sisters and nephews and nieces and I am especially happy to have Alexandra back in the family fold," said Freddie, smiling at his niece.

Lady got right to the point. "Frances is referring to your new gal pal, Freddie. Trudy Woods. You spent a lot of time with Trudy in the last two days."

"So? She is a delightful woman and a first-class tennis player. Why wouldn't I spend time with her?"

Lady put it in a nutshell, as she was so good at doing. "Freddie, we are all proud of you because you spent time with an intelligent, successful, emotionally stable woman for once in your life."

"Are you saying my ex-wives were not emotionally stable?"

"Yes, that is exactly what I am saying," said his sister bluntly. "Trudy is an improvement on the women you usually hang around."

Frances had to agree. "The women you usually pick out of a crowd to spend time with are very different from Trudy. I am glad you got to know her. Are you going to see her again?"

Freddie said, "As a matter of fact I am. I am taking her to the Miami Open to see her favorite tennis player defend his title. It should be a hoot."

Deidre changed the subject. "Freddie, your gift to Ella was so sweet. She loves the Pekingese dog that you got her and she can't wait to see it after the honeymoon."

Freddie hesitated and said, "Uh, about that. That was actually Susan's dog and er, uh, I took it back this morning."

Deidre exclaimed, "Why did you give Ella Susan's dog? I don't understand."

Freddie looked to Frances for help. Frances thought to herself, "It is Sunday. I want a break from solving problems and explaining awkward situations. I need to stop making up stories to get people out of jams." It would be too confusing to explain the dognapping, so she bailed Freddie out with another impromptu story. She explained, "Freddie planned to give Ella and Auden a puppy but could not find one in time, so he borrowed Susan's dog for the wedding, right Freddie?"

"Yes, yes. That is exactly how it happened. I am still searching for just the right Peke puppy for Ella and Auden so for the wedding I used a substitute." Freddie was relieved that he did not have to explain that he had broken into his ex-wife's house and kidnapped a dog in his backpack. His brothers would never let him live that down. But he was equally annoyed that he would now have to find a Peke breeder and buy a puppy for his niece. He brightened a little when he remembered that Trudy said her neighbor was a breeder. It would be another excuse to spend time with her.

"Well I think it was a wonderful gesture and added that special touch to the ceremony. The guests absolutely loved it. I bet we set a new trend and you will be seeing more dogs at weddings in the future," said Deidre, pleased that she had one of the first Palm Beach weddings with a dog.

Thomas broke the atmosphere of pleasant feelings by shouting to himself, "Cilantro! I told them no cilantro! Why do they put this infernal herb in every-thing nowadays?"

As he started to pick out pieces of the leafy green herb from his omelet, Frances asked, "Thomas how was your wedding date? Are you going to see Maria again?"

Thomas looked up. "Uh, what? Maria. She said it was the most interesting wedding she had ever been to what with the dog in the wedding party and the fake minister and the stolen jewelry. Despite all that, she said she had a good time and she has agreed to come see the Selby Gardens with me soon."

There was a lull in the conversation as the plates were cleared away. Frances looked across the table and observed Alexandra in lively conversation with her cousins. She noticed a distinct change in her niece from their first meeting in the lobby on Wednesday. It was not the healthy color of her skin from the Florida sun, although that was an improvement. It was not the clothes she was wearing from her new Florida wardrobe, although she looked more comfortable in a tropical climate. Frances concluded that the source of her beauty was coming from the inside. For the first time in a long time, her niece was experiencing joy.

She addressed Alexandra. "I am sorry that I could not tell you Brick's, or uh Robin's real purpose in asking you to the wedding. I knew you would be a good sport and play along. It looked like you two hit it off. Do you think you will see him again?"

Alexandra answered casually, not wanting to appear overeager. "Actually, his sister is a coach on a volleyball team in Sarasota and they need an assistant. I may help coach the team so I may see him at a tournament now and then." She did not want to talk about her love life or try to figure out her feelings toward Robin Banks, so she continued with the volleyball theme. "It is a pretty competitive team from all over the state. Since I was the backup setter at my high school, I was on the bench most of the time. I became really good at keeping stats, so that is what they want me to do at this new club. It's all about the stats on a really competitive team. I am pretty excited about it."

Thomas joined in the conversation, "What are you excited about Alexandra? Are you going to see Robin Bricks again?"

"I am excited about coaching volleyball back in Sarasota. I will probably run into Rob Banks again since his sister is a coach."

"They have a volleyball team in Sarasota?" asked Thomas.

"They have lots of teams in Florida, Dad. Both beach and indoor volleyball."

"Really? What is the difference between beach and indoor?" asked her father with a new interest in his only daughter's hobbies.

Alexandra looked at Frances and Lady, wondering if he was kidding, then politely answered, "Well, beach volleyball is played on the beach and indoor is played indoors." She added, "Beach volleyball has two players per team and indoor has six on the court."

"I can't imagine why anyone would want to spend the

weekend indoors," said Thomas. "They should be outside in nature, in a garden. You should play beach so you can be outside," said her father. After he said it, he thought how selfish and thoughtless his comment was. He would have to do better in the future in his conversations with his daughter.

"I take it that you did not go to many of Alexandra's volleyball games, Thomas," said Lady.

"We went to a few tournaments that she played in Florida, but not many," said Thomas with regret. "Brittany said they were too boring and she always got hit on the head with a flying volleyball. I have to admit, looking back, I enjoyed those moments the most." Then looking genuinely at his daughter, he said, "I'm sorry, Alexandra. I will come to your volleyball games now. I will do better."

"That's okay, Dad. I did not play very much so it was boring," said Alexandra with forgiveness in her voice.

Changing the subject away from his failure as a parent Thomas added, "I think Maria follows volleyball."

"Really, did your conversations with Maria include volleyball, Thomas?" asked Frances.

"Yes. She said that she had several nieces that played on the Puerto Rican national team and that they were coming to a tournament in Orlando next year. Imagine that. I guess nowadays they have volleyball everywhere."

The Hanlon undergrads rose early Sunday morning and filed quietly out onto the beach to watch the sunrise. They wanted to get the maximum amount of sun before they had to pile into the van to go back to North Carolina. One thing a person does not want to do is to spend a weekend in sunny Florida and not show any evidence of it on their skin. They did not want to answer the question, "If you went to Florida, why aren't you tan?" Rather, they wanted people to ask, "How did you get so tan? What did you do this weekend?" Fortunately, Florida was cooperating with their plans and provided another clear blue sky and warm sunshine. Even though it was October, the tanning index would be well above normal.

They laid their towels in a row, set their phone alarms, put on some mellow music, and began to settle in for a short nap on the beach. Harley was one of the first to place his towel on the cool sand. Without much conversation, he stretched out on his back, put on his new designer sunglasses, and closed his eyes.

Chrissy wanted to place her towel next to Harley's. This was no small gesture on her part. This is what a girl on a Florida beach does when she wants to take a step towards a relationship with a guy. She lifted her colorful beach towel up in the wind, and as she brought it down she pushed Chad out of the way with her shoulder like a roller derby queen clearing her lane. Chad fell over in the sand and complained, "Chrissy, what the heck."

At the sound of this commotion, Harley tipped his sunglasses up with one hand to watch Chrissy place her towel and sit down beside him. He tipped his glasses back over his face, closed his eyes, and smiled a jaunty smile. The undergrads would return to Hanlon minus their leader Auden Woods, but in his place a new leader of the pack had emerged—Harley Shaw.

Dylan the deejay and Lisa the caterer both felt the exhaustion mingled with relief that comes after completing a big event. Lisa had been stressed from the time she signed the contract for the biggest event of her career until the last dish was cleaned and put away. Dylan had been stressed at being asked to do such a large event with only two days' notice. Neither of them had slept much in the past few days.

Even though her head did not hit the pillow until three o'clock in the morning, Lisa rose early on Sunday. She had a sense of urgency and she grabbed a pen and paper and made a short to-do list while she drank her morning coffee. She jotted down: whiten teeth, shower, condition hair, paint fingernails, paint toenails, iron sundress, and clean sunglasses. As she jotted down her tasks, she stopped and thought, "Why am I doing all these things and why am I so nervous?"

Dylan had asked Lisa to meet him for a late breakfast at a marina near her apartment. They agreed to meet the day after the wedding because they were both too exhausted to talk after the wedding reception. She liked the café that overlooked the water near the marina, but she really did not feel like eating after working with food the preceding three days. But she did appreciate his gesture.

After completing all of the things on her list, she headed to the marina dressed in her typical Florida outfit. After moving to Florida, she had changed her look from black jeans and leather jackets to sundresses and sandals. She looked in the mirror as she walked out of her apartment and gave herself a nonverbal approval. She looked good. A girl always wants to look good when she is going to meet her old boyfriend, especially one who dumped her, showed up unexpectedly, and played "I'm sorry" songs.

Despite his late bedtime, Dylan had also gotten up early the morning after the wedding. He did not make a to-do list but rather wrote down all the things he wanted to tell Lisa that day. He wrote down all the times that he thought about her over the years. He wrote down all the things he would apologize for. He wrote down all the things he liked about her. He looked over his list and composed what amounted to a speech he wanted to give to Lisa. He thought about it when he had his morning coffee. He thought about it when he went to Publix to buy groceries. He thought about it when he made a picnic for their date.

As Lisa walked into the marina, she saw Dylan dressed in a tropical print shirt and khaki shorts and boat shoes. He smiled, took her hand and said, "I have a surprise for you." They did not walk into the café but rather walked a short distance down the dock and stopped in front of a boat that had the name "Seas the Day" printed on the back.

Lisa looked at Dylan in surprise. "You have a boat?"

"No, it belongs to a friend of mine. He never uses it. Don't ask me why. Come, let's sail away."

The boat was a top of the line craft with a very quiet motor that cut through the water without leaving much of a wake. They cruised slowly along the waterways and canals that wind throughout Fort Lauderdale. Even though the boat was quiet, they did not have a conversation while they were cruising; they just sat side-by-side enjoying the beautiful scenery. They glided past large yachts docked at large homes. They watched indigenous birds take flight as they passed by. A dolphin also followed behind in their wake, surfacing now and then.

Dylan's only words to Lisa were, "Beautiful day" and "It's a slow ride."

Once they found a quiet spot, he stopped the boat and turned off the motor. He opened the picnic basket to reveal the brunch he had prepared. He was more relaxed after the boat ride, so he spoke freely. "I know it is crazy for me to prepare food for a caterer but I thought you might get hungry."

They chatted about their lives and what had taken place since their split. He asked her about her move to Florida and her catering business. She asked him about his band, his downward spiral, getting clean, and his deejay business.

Dylan sensed that the chitchat phase of the conversation was over, and he finally got to the point of this date. He felt his stomach tighten and he became nervous again. "Lisa," he said tenderly. "Will you take a chance on me? I know I am a heartbreaker but we did have some good times. I know this may be too much, too little, and too late but I still feel for you. You are the best thing that ever happened to me."

Lisa was touched by Dylan's lyrical plea, but the pain of their breakup was still with her. She said, "I don't know Dylan. I was really hurt last time. You say you have changed, but I don't know if I can trust you again."

Dylan had no reply. She was right. She had absolutely no reason to trust him again. He bowed his head in dejected sadness and looked down at his boat shoes.

Lisa looked out over the water for a few moments, searching for more words and trying to determine her feelings. She saw a large gray bird finally take flight after dragging its feet along the water for a few seconds. She turned back to Dylan and said, "You better be good to me." Then she added with a smile, "Mama Mia! Here I go again."

THE END

Epilogue

CURRENT WRITING EXPERTS ADVISE that you should grip the reader right off the bat with an inciting incident that draws them into your plot rather than lengthy descriptions of the setting or the backstory of your characters. They say in the first few hundred words the action should take off like a scared rabbit making it impossible to put your book down. I recall reading Herman Melville and Tolstoy in high school English. I don't think anyone told them about this method, but they managed to muddle through somehow and get noticed. And another thing; aren't some readers picking up a book to escape their hectic, stressful lives? Why do I want to feed that problem?

I found it hard to follow this advice when writing my opening paragraphs. I did not want to cut descriptive paragraphs. I said to myself, "but they won't realize how great this place is that I am writing about. They won't fully understand the rich history." I could not decide if I wanted to be a bestselling author, a historian or a convention and visitors bureau. I wanted to describe in detail the beautiful setting for my book. I wanted to teach everyone about the historic landmarks in my beloved home state. I wanted the reader to put down my novel and immediately book a flight and hotel room for their next vacation.

I received feedback, probably well deserved, that the first few paragraphs of my novel sounded like a tourism pitch rather than an appropriate description of my setting. I wanted everyone to know the rich history of the area – how Henry Flagler built the railroads and brought tourism to the Palm Beach Area. I wanted everyone to read and understand the historical significance of the magnificent Breakers hotel and the Flagler Museum. I wanted them to visualize the beauty of the Japanese gardens and know the cool immigrant story behind it.

I decided to defer to the advice of the more learned and have omitted much detail in my descriptions of place. However, as far as I know, there are no rules against adding a chapter at the end. I would encourage you to read the following paragraphs and continue to learn the history of the places mentioned. That way I will feel better; that I have done my job and you have appropriately appreciated one of the most beautiful and interesting places in the world.

The Breakers
www.thebreakers.com

On the shores of the Atlantic Ocean, on the southeast coast of Florida sits the majestic Breakers Palm Beach resort spreading out on acres of lush oceanfront property. This grand hotel built by industrial and railroad tycoon, Henry Morrison Flagler, was so named because guests often requested rooms "down by the breakers" indicating rooms closest to the breaking waves of the ocean. In the height of the Gilded Age, Flagler extended the East Coast Railroad and built luxurious hotels opening up this sparsely settled part of southeast Florida and providing wealthy tourists a tropical paradise to escape harsh winters in the north.

Alachua County

Alachua County in northern Florida is probably best known for the City of Gainesville – home to the University of Florida. This area is quite different from the typical beaches and theme parks that draw visitors. It has small towns, large live oaks, cattle and horse farms, and natural springs. Another claim to fame is being the birthplace of rock star Tom Petty. This son of Florida, born in Gainesville, rose to fame selling millions of albums.

Worth Avenue, Palm Beach

www.worth-avenue.com

This Mediterranean Revival-style shopping and dining area built by Addison Mizner in the early 1900s, is a delightful place to stroll and grab a bite to eat, whether you are in the top one percent of the country's wealthy or fall somewhere below that. The palm-tree-lined streets are filled with high-end shops, art galleries and restaurants. There are boutiques and cafes tucked into European-style courtyards with bubbling fountains. Lush flowering vines climb up buildings and container gardens spill over with flowering plants.

Morikami Museum and Japanese Gardens
www.morikami.org

Morikami Gardens, near Delray Beach, was founded by a group of pioneering Japanese farmers in the early twentieth century. The Yamato Colony, as it was called, was finally abandoned but the gardens and the cultural museum remain.

Flagler Museum
www.flaglermuseum.us

Henry Flagler built the seventy-five-room, Beaux Arts style mansion as a wedding present for his wife Mary Lily Keenan. Whitehall, as it was called during the height of the Gilded Age, is set on the shores of Lake Worth. Henry Flagler's personal railcar is housed in the Pavilion that is fashioned after a turn of the century railway station.

A Note from the Author:

I hope you have as much fun reading this book as I had writing it. This is my first book in the *Thank God It's Friday Series* and I plan to write many more. I am a native Floridian who loves all things about the sunshine state. I live close to the beach and never want to move.

If you would like to find out more please connect with me via my website

www.mnvollmer.com

Made in the USA
Coppell, TX
30 May 2021

56597115R00154